THE
GAS STATION
GIRL

A story of recovery from sex trafficking

Jensen Siblings Book 2

Todd H. Davis

Contents

Prologue

The dark-haired girl in denim shorts and red cropped tank top slipped out of the motel room when her handler was distracted by a customer. The effects of the roofie were already starting to cloud her mind, but she had rehearsed this in her head so often, she operated on instinct. She ran in her bare feet across the parking lot to a row of bushes near the street. From that vantage point, she surveyed the parking lot for a possible means of escape and for anyone who might force her back. Sedans and pickup trucks were lined up in the favored spaces in front of the motel. Many were backed into the spaces to make for an easy getaway. She spotted a pickup truck parked head-in, meaning she could climb into the back without detection from anyone looking out from a motel room window. Even better, it had a large toolbox mounted across the bed behind the cab.

With one more glance around the area to ensure no one was watching, she ran to the back of the truck and climbed in. Keeping her head down, she scooted into the narrow space between the bottom of the tool box and the floor of the truck bed. Then she waited. After several minutes, she heard the voices of several men who had come out looking for her. She heard her handler giving orders to others to search in different directions. Then she felt a slight motion as someone leaned on the truck, presumably looking into the bed, then inside the cab. He apparently didn't spot her hiding under the toolbox. After a few calls of "Nothing" and "Damn", the girl heard the men enter one of the motel rooms and close the door.

At some point, she fell asleep, whether due to the drugs she had been forced to take or the tiredness that followed the adrenalin rush of the escape. She awakened when the truck pulled into a gas station. Her mind felt foggy and she couldn't remember why she lay in the back of a truck; only that she needed to get away from it. While the driver inserted his credit card into the pump, she climbed out over the opposite side and sat down on the pavement behind a trash can, well within view of other patrons of the gas station, but out of sight of the driver of the pickup truck that brought her there. She believed the others weren't a danger to her, only the man in the pickup, but she didn't know why she believed that. Her clouded brain couldn't reason it out.

Once the pickup pulled away, she stood up shakily, swaying a bit. Someone called out to her. Not in anger or aggression. Was it concern? She stumbled to a car whose driver was putting away the fuel nozzle and tried to open the back door. In her inebriated state, she couldn't quite grasp the handle, but stumbled and fell to the pavement in a sort of slow-motion fall. A young Black man next to a large black SUV talked on his phone and watched her at the same time. From her position on the pavement, she flopped over face down and pushed her hands against the concrete to lift the upper part of her body, and then slid her knees forward so she was on all fours. She slowly, awkwardly rose from that position and looked at the man on the phone.

She tried to open the back door of his SUV, but it was locked. Perhaps the man had locked it after watching her try to get into the sedan. He called out to her; was he asking if she needed help? In her clouded state of mind, she didn't understand what he said, nor could she respond coherently. She tried another door of the SUV. Also locked. The SUV driver held the phone out in front of him, in her direction. He called out to her again with different words. She had no better comprehension this time than the last. Then he walked up to her, to the back door that she had tried to open. After a double beep sounded, he opened the door and stood back, looking at her. He spoke more words that had a familiarity, but which she still couldn't grasp. She only knew that the vehicle would take her someplace away from the circumstances she had run away from. She got into the vehicle and he reached in and fastened her seat belt.

The driver removed the fuel nozzle and placed it back on the pump to complete the transaction. Other patrons of the gas station watched the entire encounter with a variety of thoughts: annoyance, amusement, disgust, concern. Whether for good or for bad, only the driver of the black SUV had taken action. The young man climbed into the driver's seat, started the engine, and drove away.

Chapter 1
The girl

"Hey, John, can you give me a ride home?"

"Sure thing, Jaxon. You didn't drive the MomMobile today?"

"I *got* here in the MomMobile. It's just that it left without me." The MomMobile referred to a white minivan with a vanity license plate that said 'MARA MOM'.

"Wait, wait, wait. You mean your mom dropped you off at the stadium?" Chris asked as he dropped the trash from his meal in the bin on the way out of the restaurant.

"Yeah. I know. I feel like I'm the only eleventh grader who doesn't have a set of wheels," Jaxon replied before slurping the remainder of his drink.

"I don't care about that. So, Marathon Mom was at the football game and didn't come by to say Hi to us. Then she drove you here to Tico's Tacos, and still didn't come in? I'm disappointed," Chris stated, pouting.

"You should see her out on the jogging trail in her running shorts and sports bra," Chris told Kevin in a faux whisper.

"Ugh. Stop." Jaxon rolled his eyes. "You're talking about my mom. I just need a ride home."

"Well, it's a good thing I have room in the battleship," John stated, referring to his black Cadillac Escalade ESV. It was technically the family car, but he was the only one in the family to use it daily. His sister and brother-in-law only used it for family trips that required luggage space or when shuttling the family plus friends to some event, much like John was doing now. The friends who didn't have their own vehicles, or just didn't want to drive in the after-game traffic, could depend on John for a lift.

"After Chris' stupid comments about my mom, I should get to ride in the front, away from him," Jaxon stated.

"That's not gonna happen," Keona commented, pointing with her thumb to a dark-haired girl with side ponytails.

"Oh. Sorry, Lizzie."

"Come on Jaxon, you can sit with me in the back," Nicole offered.

"Aw, Niki," Chris exclaimed, "You're ditching me for Jaxon?"

"Yeah, Chris. You just stated a preference for older women and I don't think I fit that demographic. And it's 'Nicole'; I haven't gone by Niki since middle school. You're the only one who still calls me that."

"Well, Jaxon's shorter than you."

"Most of the guys are shorter than me, but I don't see how that matters for a ride home."

"I like tall girls," Jaxon stated. "I mean, it's not a fetish or anything, I just …"

"Shh. Stop talking about my height or I'll trade you for Kevin."

As the group approached the Escalade, the kids lined up at the back doors while John walked Lizzie Abboud to the front passenger door and double-clicked the remote to unlock the door just as he reached for the handle.

Although the football game and late-night meal were done as a group, Lizzie was always the last one he drove home, regardless of where the other passengers lived. She was also the only passenger he walked to the front door.

"Is your father watching?" John asked when they stepped up to her door.

"You always ask that. He probably is." Lizzie pointed to the doorbell camera.

John waved into the camera and then positioned himself to block the view while he kissed Lizzie good night.

A voice came through the doorbell speaker. "Stop blocking the camera, John."

"Hi, Dr. Abboud. Just saying good night," John said as he stepped away from the camera.

"Can you see us now, Baba?"

"Yes, Lizzie. Thank you."

She leaned toward John on her tiptoes and gave him another kiss.

"Hey, hey, hey! None of that," called the voice on the speaker.

"Oh, I thought you wanted to watch," Lizzie stated with a giggle.

"Baba actually likes you," she told John from the open doorway. "He looks forward to having you on his crew for the church service projects."

"Don't give away my secrets," came the voice from the speaker.

* * *

After John left Lizzie, the vehicle's fuel sensor chimed. It had enough gas for the trip home, but he decided to fuel up right away. He pulled into the Exxon station near the freeway. Even at eleven-thirty at night, the gas station had several customers. As he took the spot of a pickup that pulled away, he noticed a dark-haired woman – girl? – sitting on the ground against a trash bin. John looked toward the convenience store. *She must be waiting for a friend in the store*, he thought. It also registered with him that she looked kind of cute in her denim shorts and red cropped tank top.

John swiped his credit card, inserted the fuel nozzle into the SUV and set it to pump on its own. While waiting for the tank to fill, he called Sophie – his twenty-year-old sister and legal guardian since his parents passed away three years ago – to report that he'd stopped for gas. Sophie could check his location on the tracking app all the family members had on their phones, but she still insisted he call at night if he deviated from his usual route, such as stopping for gas.

The girl behind the trash bin rose on wobbly legs and stumbled to a nearby sports car. *Nice car*, John thought. *Don't know why she'd sit on the ground instead of her car.* She tried the handle of the passenger door, but it was locked. John looked back at the store, expecting her friend to appear at any moment. However, she then walked shakily to an older model sedan with a little stick figure family on the back window. A chubby man removed the pump nozzle from the sedan when the girl tried to open the back door. The man yelled, "Hey! Get away!"

"What was that?" Sophie asked.

"There's a girl here acting weird. She tried to get in someone's car and she's walking funny, like she's drunk." He watched as she stumbled away from the car and slowly sank to the pavement.

"She's on the ground now."

"Put me on FaceTime," Sophie commanded.

John changed the call to a FaceTime session and pointed the camera at the girl.

The chubby man quickly got into his sedan and locked the doors, soon pulling away and leaving the girl behind. Sophie and John watched the girl flop over onto her stomach and push both hands against the pavement to raise her upper body. She then slid her knees forward and pushed with her feet to lift her backside off the floor, now on all fours. John then noticed her bare feet.

"All the cars that were here when I first came are gone now. So I don't think she's waiting for someone."

The scene would have been comical if it weren't for John's concern for the girl's safety. The girl turned her attention to John's Escalade. John quickly locked the doors with the remote key fob as she tried to open the back driver's side door.

"John, ask her if she needs help."

"Hey, do you need help?" John called out.

She looked up and mumbled something incoherent before shakily walking around to the other side of the SUV to try the other back door. She put her face to the window as if looking inside.

"I don't think she's regular drunk," Sophie said. "I think she's in some sort of trouble and you can't leave her there. Some creep will come along and pick her up and we'll see her story on an episode of 'America's Unsolved Crimes'."

"So, what should I do?"

"Open the door for her," Sophie commanded. "If she gets in, bring her here. If she doesn't, call 9-1-1 and let the police handle it."

John double-clicked the remote to unlock the doors. He went to the back door nearest the girl and opened it. "If you want to get in, go ahead. We'll try to help you," he said. Without even looking at him, she climbed into the vehicle and sat in the middle of the second row. John reached in and buckled her seat belt, then closed the door. If other patrons at the gas station were watching, he didn't notice. He climbed into the driver seat, started the engine, and drove home.

* * *

"Explain this to me again," Ty asked his wife. "John's bringing a stranger home? And we're gonna do what?"

"John found a girl wandering around the gas station like she's drunk or on drugs."

"Or mentally ill," Ty added.

"Maybe, but he couldn't just leave her there. She needs help. She can sleep it off here and then we can take her home or let her call someone to come get her."

"And you don't think the sheriff's department could handle it?"

"They deal with criminals. She looked more like a victim than a criminal. She doesn't need a police record just for being drunk or high or whatever."

"Sophie, this sounds dangerous. She could be a drug addict or a mental case."

At home, Sophie and her husband Ty met the Escalade as it pulled up. The girl had dozed off or passed out, depending on how you looked at it. As Sophie opened the door and leaned in to unfasten the seat belt, the mystery girl stirred, but seemed to lack full control over her own body.

"Does she look dangerous to you?" Sophie asked Ty.

He shrugged. "I still think it's a bad idea."

Sophie had to drag the girl to the edge of the seat where John and Ty could lift her out. With one on each side, they half carried, half walked her into the house, and sat her on the sofa.

"What's your name?" Sophie asked.

The girl looked up at Sophie before closing her eyes and dropping her head down. Ty tapped her on her shoulder.

"Hey, hey, wake up."

She looked up at Ty with her eyes while her head still hung down. Ty knelt down to her level.

"*¿Cómo te llamas?*" Ty asked in Spanish.

She closed her eyes again.

"What if she goes into a coma or dies in her sleep?" Ty asked, looking at Sophie.

Fourteen-year-old Emi stepped up and put her fingers on the girl's neck. Then she put the fingers of her other hand on her own neck.

"What are you doing?" John asked.

"Comparing her pulse to mine. Hers is a little slower, but not that slow. I don't think she's gonna die."

"You're not a doctor. We don't know what she's on and how it's affected her," Ty asserted.

"I think it's a date rape drug," Sophie stated.

The others looked at her.

"Then we need to get her to a hospital and get the sheriff's department involved," Ty pointed out.

"Okay. You're right," Sophie stated. "Let's get her back to the Escalade."

"How's she doing back there?" Ty asked from the driver's seat on the way to the hospital.

"She's still alive," Sophie stated sarcastically. "Groggy."

"Not sleeping?"

"Tired," the girl said with slurred speech.

11

"She said something!" Emi exclaimed from her position next to the girl and behind Ty.

"Are you awake?" Emi asked.

"Tired."

"We think you've been drugged. We're taking you to the hospital," Sophie stated.

The girl leaned to her right, toward Sophie. "You're pretty. Don' nee' ho'pital. Tired."

"You need help. They'll make sure you're okay."

"No hospital. Jus' nee' sleep."

"See, we're already here," Sophie said. The bright lights above the emergency room doors illuminated the vehicle.

"NO HOSPITAL!" Her pronunciation was still slurred, but the message was clear.

After setting the gear in park, Ty turned around to look at the girl and then at Sophie.

The girl looked at Ty. "I go wi' you."

"Well, I'm going into the hospital."

She turned toward Sophie. "Ca' I go wi' you?"

"I don't think she wants to go to the hospital," John stated.

"Or you," the girl said, pointing clumsily at John.

"Maybe we should just go back home," Emi said.

"You' pretty, too. Are you working?" the girl asked Emi.

"She may be drugged or drunk or whatever," Sophie said, "but she seems to be aware enough to know she doesn't want to go to the hospital."

"No hospital. Jus' sleep."

"Ty, let's go home," Sophie directed

"We're already here. We might as well…"

"Ty. Take us home." It was an order.

Ty sighed heavily as he put the vehicle into gear and pulled away from the emergency room entrance. "I've got a bad feeling about this," he muttered to himself.

By the time they returned home, the girl was sleeping again. Sophie again pulled her to the edge of the seat for Ty and John to lift her out.

"Sofa again?"

"No," Sophie stated. "She needs a real bed. Take her upstairs to my old room." It was the room Sophie had before she married Ty and moved into the master bedroom with him downstairs.

The stairs were too narrow for Ty and John to maneuver while carrying the girl between them. At the bottom of the stairs, John turned to look at Ty.

"I've got this."

"What do you mean?" Ty asked.

"I've got her." With his left hand around her back, John reached down with his right hand behind the girl's knees and lifted her into a bridal hold.

"You're gonna drop her," Emi warned.

John carried the girl upstairs and laid her on the bed in Sophie's old room. He turned to Emi. "I didn't drop her," he stated smugly.

Emi set out a new toothbrush, still in the package, and a small tube of toothpaste, next to the sink in the bathroom that connected her room with the newly designated guest room. The toothbrush and toothpaste were promotional items from her dentist on her last visit. Upon seeing the girl's dirty feet before they pulled the covers up over her, Emi returned to the bathroom and placed a fresh towel and washcloth next to the sink.

"Are you gonna put a mint on her pillow, too?" Ty asked.

"What does that mean?" Emi replied.

"He thinks you're making this like a hotel," John commented.

"Oh, yeah. One more thing." Emi ran downstairs to the teddy bear collection in the living room. She selected one that had diminishing sentimental value, went back upstairs to the guest room, and placed it on the bed next to their sleeping visitor.

"Another 'one more thing'," Sophie declared. "She'll need clean clothes." She looked at Emi. "She looks a bit skinny. I think my pants will be too big for her. Can you lend her some clothes?"

"Okay."

Although now quite late, John and Lizzie exchanged text messages about the entire ordeal. Lizzie initially responded, "Right after our date, you picked up another girl? Was our date that bad?" She finished the message with, "LOL."

Chapter 2
Awake

What is this place? Still lying in bed, the girl looked around the unfamiliar room. *It's obviously a bedroom and I'm the only one in it. It's bigger than my bedroom in my parents' house; bigger than the room I share with the other girls. No mattresses on the floor.*

She pulled back the covers and sat up, noticing her attire. *I'm wearing my street clothes.* She stood up and looked around the room again. A portrait of a bride and groom hung on the wall above the bed. A Black woman and a White man. A small engraved plate on the bottom of the frame identified the subjects as William and Esther Jensen. Not recent. The date under the names indicated a wedding from over two decades ago.

She walked to the window and peered out onto the scene outside. From her position, it was clear she was on the second floor of a house. She saw two-story brick houses across the street, larger than the one she grew up in. A middle-aged White couple worked in the flower bed of the house across the street and a Black teenaged boy mowed the lawn to the left of that one. An Asian woman pushed a stroller down the sidewalk in front of the girl's window. *Looks like a suburb. A nice suburb. Am I still in Katy?*

On the wall opposite the window was a closed door. She quietly opened the door to see a hallway and what looked like a railing overlooking a large open room. She quietly closed the door again and turned her attention to an opening next to the bed. She saw a sink through the opening. A bathroom.

Where there's a sink, there's got to be a toilet; and I could use a toilet right now.

A door off the side of the sink area led to the toilet and bathtub. She could see an open door on the opposite side of the bathroom. *This house is much nicer than the other one*, she thought. Before taking advantage of the toilet, she ventured to the other door. Another sink. Another bedroom. It had an occupant.

In addition to a giant teddy bear sitting up on the bed, a girl with black hair pulled up into a large puff of tight coils sat at a desk, her back to the bathroom. *African American. Maybe she's related to the couple in the wedding portrait.*

The house guest carefully closed the door between the toilet area and the other bedroom and locked it.

At about 10:00 am, the family members received a text.

> Emi:
> She's awake.

The sound of a flushing toilet had prompted the text. It was a bizarre sort of entertainment event. Everyone had been waiting to find out the identity of the mysterious gas station girl and had been sensitive to her awakening. John rearranged his lawn mowing schedule and Ty delayed a visit to the hardware store so they could be on hand for her emergence. With Emi's news, the family gathered at the table in the informal dining area between the kitchen and the family room trying to act nonchalant.

When she finally emerged from the bedroom, she stood at the upstairs balcony that overlooked the living room and kitchen table area. She wore the same clothes that she had arrived in, with hair a little disheveled.

"Good morning!" Sophie called out. "Would you like breakfast? We have eggs and bacon."

"You didn't offer that to us," John whispered.

"Shh," Emi scolded.

"What is this place, and who are you?" the girl asked; a little harshly, thought several of the family members. At least some recognized that the "you" probably referred to the group, not specifically to Sophie.

"I'm Sophie and that's my husband Ty," she said, pointing to Ty. Ty waved. "And this is our house. That's my brother John who found you and brought you home last night," she said pointing to John, who followed Ty's lead and also waved. "And that's my sister Emi," she finished, pointing to her sister.

"Hi. I'm in the room next to yours. We share a bathroom," Emi explained in greeting. "We forgot to lay out a hairbrush," she whispered to the group.

"Come on down and let me get you some breakfast. Eggs and bacon?" Sophie repeated.

"No bacon," the girl responded before descending the stairs. Sophie assumed that meant she wanted the eggs. Ty stood up to help in the kitchen. He put two slices of bread into the toaster and poured orange juice into a glass.

The girl walked slowly down the stairs to get a look at the photos attached to the stairway wall. She recognized some of the faces as those of the people who just greeted her. Most were of vacations, holidays, and other special occasions and none included the couple from the bedroom portrait. The stairs pointed towards the front door, so the girl had to walk through the entry hall and living room, with its windows overlooking the backyard, to get to the informal dining area. She paused to look down a short hallway off of the entry hall and saw, on the wall at the end, a portrait of a Black woman and White man. *Is that the same couple as in the picture upstairs? They look older in this one.* The two-story living room had a fireplace with four teddy bears sitting on its mantle and a low-profile console piano to one side. More teddy bears were scattered among bookshelves on either side of the fireplace. *Someone must like teddy bears a lot. Maybe that girl in the other bedroom. Did they say her name is Emi? She had that huge bear on her bed.* She glanced around once more before arriving at the table. *This house is bigger than my parents' house; bigger than the house I just left. Nicer, too. With real furniture.*

The mystery girl stood by the table, warily looking around the room, unsure of whether she could trust these strangers. *How did I get here?* she wondered. Quickly surmising that the people posed no immediate danger, she sat down at the table across from John. Ty set down the glass of orange juice and a glass of water in front of her.

"What's your name?" Ty asked. She didn't respond but downed the whole glass of orange juice.

"Okay. You can tell us your name later, but we eventually need to call you something besides 'hey you'. Do you remember anything from last night?"

The girl hesitated before shaking her head 'no'. She finally said, "You can call me Allie."

"Welcome to our home, Allie. John, why don't you explain how you found her last night?"

John proceeded to describe Allie's behavior at the gas station and the family's decision to bring her home. He described the stumbling, the attempts to get into strangers' cars, and her eventual arrival at their house.

"We laid out the toothbrush, towels, and clothes for you. We forgot a hairbrush, though," Emi explained. Allie self-consciously ran her fingers through her hair in an attempt to smooth it down. "After breakfast, you may want to shower and change. Your clothes are kind of dirty."

"Emi!" John reprimanded.

"Thank you," Allie said, keeping with the pattern of short responses.

"Allie, do you want to call someone? You can use my phone," Ty said and laid his phone on the table in front of her and then took a step back. Sophie scooted the phone to the side as she put the plate of eggs and toast on the table in its place.

"I have a headache," Allie stated. She picked up a slice of toast and started eating while looking at the phone. Presently, she replied to the question. "I don't want to call anyone."

Ty found the bottle of ibuprofen and set it down in front of their guest, then went back to the kitchen to start washing the egg pan and spatula. John and Emi continued sitting at the table, pretending to check their phones for updates from friends. Sophie surveyed the situation as she sat down at the table. "Allie, is there anything you can tell us about who you are and how you got to the gas station?"

"Yeah, this is the most exciting thing we've had in months. We all want to know what happened," Emi stated bluntly.

Allie finished her meal in silence.

"You know what?" Ty said. "I think Emi, John, and I need to get out of the way so we don't overwhelm Allie."

As they left the table, Ty teased Emi, "What do you mean this is the most exciting thing in months? Are you forgetting all the drama we had this year? Do you think this is more exciting than our big banquet a couple of weeks ago and more exciting than Aunt Ruth's wedding in Hawaii in the summer? And, frankly, I put the adoption way up there in the excitement category."

Ty's first reference was to the party that took place only a few days before, a combination of Sophie's birthday celebration and delayed wedding reception. He and Sophie were married in March but didn't have a public celebration of it until Sophie turned twenty. His last reference was about when John and Emi surprised him with adoption papers during the court proceedings that transferred legal guardianship from the kids' grandmother in Dallas to their older sister Sophie. The adoption made him a co-guardian with Sophie and brought him to tears at their act of endearment.

Just before Ty led Emi and John outside, Sophie had to interject her own thoughts. "Hey, higher than our wedding?" she called out. "That should be top on your list of excitement."

"It's up there, but the very top of my list is our first night on the honeymoon. It'll be hard to top that."

"Eww," Emi said, putting her hands over her ears. "I don't need to hear that." John just shook his head as they exited the house and closed the door.

"Allie, it looked like you were drugged last night," Sophie stated. "If you were raped, we need to report it to the police and get you tested. I had a seminar at school about date rape. They said you should preserve your clothes for evidence and shouldn't clean yourself until they get samples."

Allie stared at the fork in her hand and rubbed its embossed design with her thumb. "I *was* drugged, but it's not what you think. I don't need to call the police or save any evidence."

"Do you remember us taking you to the hospital?"

"No. I didn't need a hospital. Did the hospital just let me go?"

"No. You were pretty adamant that you didn't want to go in, so we came back home."

"I don't remember much about last night, but I can guess what happened. I'd been planning to leave for a while and even thought of how to do it. I'd wait for a distraction at the motel, then sneak out and hide in the back of a truck. I thought once I got away, I'd jump out of the truck. So, that's probably how I got to the gas station."

"Wait. Back up. Motel? Do you live at a motel?"

Allie wondered if she'd already said too much. Could she trust this woman with more details? Would she call the police? She sat in silence for several seconds while deciding if she should say more.

"Allie, look, we suspect you're in some kind of trouble and we want to help," Sophie explained. "My husband wanted to call the police, but I thought we should hear from you first."

"Please don't call the police," Allie pleaded. "I ran away from home and got mixed up with some bad people." She hesitated to tell her the rest. She looked out the window and saw the other family members standing on the patio, frequently glancing in through the window.

After hearing the banter among the family members as they went outside, Allie decided they meant no harm to her.

"They can come back in. I know you're gonna tell them everything I say anyway."

"Are you sure?"

Allie nodded and Sophie waved for the family to come back in.

Sophie summarized the getaway story for the family before turning back to Allie. "How old are you?"

"Seventeen. I'll be eighteen in January. If you call the police, they'll send me back home."

"And I take it you don't want to go back?"

"I ran away from my father last year. He wanted me to live my life a certain way and I didn't. After what I've done, if you send me back, he'll probably kill me; and I mean literally."

"What've you done?"

She again sat quietly for several awkward seconds, rubbing the fork and pondering how much to tell these strangers. *Allie, you didn't think this through*, she told herself. *What did you think would happen after you got away? Hitchhike to a homeless shelter?*

"I ran away with a guy I met online. He was nice at first, but later…" She looked down and took a deep breath. "I'm a prostitute."

"You're seventeen," Ty stated. "You're not a prostitute, you're a rape victim."

"Whatever you call it, men pay money to fu…," she stopped mid-sentence and looked around at the family, "…uh…to have sex with me.

"So anyway, I don't live at the motel. I live – lived – in a house with other girls like me and a couple of… uh…

23

handlers. They'd take us to the motel at night to meet the… uh… customers." She continued, "I tried to leave a couple of weeks ago and didn't make it. They beat me to send a message. Then they started giving me roofies to make me more… um… relaxed and…uh… cooperative."

The room became quiet as the severity of Allie's experience settled onto the family. Sophie looked at Ty and he could almost read her thoughts. *I must be getting good at this,* he thought. *Perhaps that's what happens when you're with people for three years.* He gave a slight nod to Sophie.

Sophie finally broke the silence. "We'll help you. You can stay with us while you sort out what you need."

"But Allie," Ty started. "We need to know that you are who you say you are. We want to be able to trust that if we open our home to you, you're not gonna rob us. My name's Tyler Butler. I go by Ty. You can walk outside our house and see the house number; walk to the corner and see the name of our street. My parents live three houses down. That way," he said pointing.

"There. You now know more about me than we know about you. Is 'Allie' short for something? Allison, Alicia, Alexa? What's your full name? Where are you from?"

"I don't want to say. I'm afraid you'll call the police and they'll send me back to my parents." She looked at Sophie. "Please let me stay. I won't rob you."

"Okay," Sophie said. "Emi left some clothes for you in your bedroom. Since you don't want to save anything for evidence, we can wash your clothes after you change. Why don't you go upstairs and shower while we figure out how to make this work."

"Thank you," she directed to Sophie. She looked at Ty and repeated, "Thank you."

As everyone stood up from the table, they could see that seventeen-year-old Allie appeared to be about the same size and height as fourteen-year-old Emi at five-foot-two. However, the similarities stopped there. Emi's dark complexion and tight curly black hair were in contrast to Allie's lighter skin and long slightly wavy hair. They hoped Emi's clothes would fit.

* * *

Once they heard the water running in the shower, the Butler and Jensen family reconvened at the kitchen table.

"There are agencies that deal with this kind of thing: runaways and sex trafficking," Ty stated. "We don't have any experience with this. If someone reports us hiding a runaway kid, would we get in trouble?"

"She said she'll be eighteen in January, so it's only three months," Sophie pointed out.

"Only three months that we help her or only three months of risk getting caught hiding a runaway?" Ty asked.

"You make it sound so bad. She's a scared seventeen-year-old who needs help and probably doesn't even know what kind of help she needs. I used to be a scared seventeen-year-old who needed help and you were there for me."

"I think we helped each other."

Sophie rose to take Allie's plate to the kitchen. "She needs help and we can give it to her. Help to get her life back, even if it takes more than three months. We have the extra bedroom," she pleaded.

"Her story made me want to cry," Emi stated.

"I want to trust her," Ty continued, "but before we let a stranger stay with us, I'd be more comfortable if we could do a background check. How do we know she's even seventeen? What if she's fourteen? If what she's telling us is true, I do want to help her, but how do we know she's not some kind of con artist who'll call her friends to come to steal everything in the house when I go off to work and y'all leave for school?"

The discussion went quiet as they pondered that thought.

"As long as one of us is here, she can't do that, right?" Emi asked. "What if she has to leave the house when we leave the house? She could hang out in the backyard....Or...She could stay in your camper while we're gone."

"Ty?" Sophie asked.

"That's a good idea, Emi. There's nothing worth stealing in there."

"We're gonna have to budget for her," John stated. John held the role of family accountant, keeping track of the family finances and leading monthly budget meetings. "The food and clothing expenses are gonna go up."

"Ty," Sophie said softly, reaching out for his hand.

"Yeah?"

"Are you okay with this? You brought up a lot of concerns. You know my position, but I'll defer to your judgment."

John and Emi looked at each other with raised eyebrows. The idea of Sophie voluntarily deferring to someone was a new concept. Maybe marriage had a positive effect on her.

"I just wanted to make sure we all understand the risk and cost involved," Ty said, "but, yeah, I'm okay with it."

"Me, too," Emi added.

"And me," said John.

When Allie emerged from her bedroom, freshly showered and clothed, Sophie met her at the bottom of the stairs with a pair of Emi's flip-flops, "Let's go shopping to get you some basic necessities."

"Can I come?" Emi asked.

"Sure."

"I'm coming, too," John stated.

"Don't you have lawns to mow?" Ty asked. "I don't think they'll be shopping for anything you'd be interested in."

"At least get me more shaving gel. I'm almost out."

* * *

"Can we have a family game night?" Emi asked after dinner.

"I was gonna hang out with the guys, but I can do a game night," John stated. Ty and Sophie looked at each other with smirks. John had passed the age where he enjoyed a family game night. He merely tolerated the game nights they had after their monthly family budget meetings.

He just wants to see if Allie reveals any more about her life, Sophie thought.

The family settled on the card game 'Uno'. Allie stood at the threshold between the living room and the informal dining area where the family members were seating themselves around the table. Ty shuffled the cards and started to deal them out for five players.

"Are you gonna join us, Allie?" Sophie asked.

"I don't know how to play. I'll just watch."

"It's easy, I can show you," Emi stated.

"You guys can play. I'll watch," Allie restated.

Ty gathered the extra pile of cards and placed them at the bottom of the draw pile. After each player had taken two turns, Ty looked up to see Allie still standing on the threshold, as if uncertain as to which room she wanted to be in.

"Allie," he stated.

She looked at him but didn't answer.

"Since you're not playing, can you get me a glass of iced tea? The glasses are in the upper cabinet to the left of the sink and the tea's in the fridge."

"Sure."

Sophie gave Ty a puzzled look and Ty just gave her a smile in return. "At least I got her moving," he whispered.

Upon bringing the tea, Ty stated, "Thank you. Why don't you have a seat between John and Emi."

Ty halfway expected a protest, but she obediently sat down in the empty chair between John and Emi and continued to observe the family and the game.

"How many lawns did you mow today, John?" Sophie asked.

"I did one before…. One this morning and then three more in the afternoon. I had planned for one more but ran out of time. I'll do that one tomorrow after church."

"That'll pay for a few dates with Lizzie," Sophie said.

"I'm thinking more like Rockets tickets and gas for the battleship," John replied. "That's what I call the SUV," John explained to Allie.

"Allie, what do you do in your spare time?" Sophie asked.

Allie shrugged her shoulders. "Watch TV, read." She kept her answers short and Sophie didn't press further.

By the end of the third round of 'Uno', the family gave up hope that Allie would join the game. They finally called it a night and the family members retired to their rooms, including Allie to the guest room.

* * *

At the end of the evening, after Ty and Sophie walked through the downstairs areas to turn off the lights and make sure the doors were locked, Ty shouted "Good night" to the household. Emi's and John's muffled replies were heard from behind their closed doors. Only Allie came out of her room to the banister overlooking the living room and called back clearly, "Thank you for everything. Good night." Ty and Sophie realized that she was in the process of changing into sleepwear when she'd heard Ty's call, because when she came out to reply, she was topless, holding her sleeping shirt in her hand.

"Was she....?" Ty asked, without finishing the question.

"Yes," Sophie replied as she grabbed Ty's hand and pulled him towards their bedroom. "But I'll make you forget what you saw."

* * *

The light was dim in the forest, bright enough to avoid trees, but dark enough to enhance her feeling of dread. She was running, as she had so many times. She knew she shouldn't look back. Doing so would slow her down, or, worse, she could stumble over a fallen branch and fall. If that happened, the wolves would be on her in no time. Just keep running. She could already feel their breath on her neck, but it may have been her imagination because the sound of their leaps indicated they were still several yards back. All she could think was 'run'. She saw something up ahead. An open doorway. In the forest. A cabin? The area around the door was dark, but light shined from the doorway like a beacon. She ran.

Allie awoke with a start, her heart beating fast, body damp with sweat. It was still dark outside. She felt for the old phone Ty had given her last night and tapped the screen to see the time. 3:12 am. She'd had this dream many times over the past several months, or variation of it, at least. The locations changed: forest, dark alley, desert wilderness. And the predators changed: wolves, angry men, unseen monsters. A couple of times it was a giant wheel, bearing down to crush her. The doorway. Her previous dreams didn't have a doorway. She had always run away from something, never toward something.

Chapter 3
Sunday lunch

Sunday morning, Ty called out a morning greeting meant to remind the crew to wake up and get ready for church. Allie, being unsure of the family's morning rituals, also got up and got dressed. The family prepared cold cereal and toast for themselves, getting their own bowls, spoons, and cups from the cabinets. Allie watched and followed suit. She also noticed the Bibles that the family members had placed on the table while they prepared breakfast.

"Good morning, Allie," John called out. "We're getting ready to go to church."

Allie was unsure what that meant for her. *Will they force me to go with them? If not, I'll have to go to the trailer while they're gone, as agreed yesterday.*

"We'd love for you to go with us," Ty stated. "But you're under no obligation. If you come with us, we may eat at a restaurant afterward. If not, we'll just order out and bring it home."

"I, uh, would just rather stay here this time. Maybe next week," she replied.

"Okay. The service will be over at about twelve-fifteen and we'll be home about one o'clock after picking up lunch," Ty stated. "Do you still have my mom's old phone?"

Allie held it up.

"Good. Remember, it doesn't have cell service, so you can't make regular phone calls, only 9-1-1 if you have an emergency. However, you can connect to the home wifi and get to the internet. I installed ChatUsUp on it yesterday so we can text each other. I'm sending you a test message."

Ty tapped out a message on his phone. The phone in Allie's hand chimed in response.

"I got it."

"I'll text you when we're on the way home. You have all our contacts and my parents' info, too, so if anything comes up, you can text any of us."

"Thank you."

"If you're looking for something to do, I recommend walking around the neighborhood and getting familiar with it. Or you can grab a book from the bookcase in the upstairs den before we leave."

"Okay. I'll be fine. And I won't steal anything."

"Did you text her about stealing?" Sophie asked Ty.

"No, I just said 'Hi'."

"I just meant it as a joke," Allie explained.

She was glad they didn't pressure her to go to church with them. She still hadn't determined if their kindness was sincere or a cover for something sinister. *What if they're part of some kind of religious cult?"* she wondered. The fact that they didn't pressure her to go with them was a good sign. If they continued to behave normally throughout the week, she might consider going to church with them next Sunday. She had never seen a Christian church service and thought it might at least be educational.

About one o'clock the family showed up with a bag of burritos. Another car pulled up behind them in the driveway and a young woman got out, also carrying a bag. Allie rose from her position in one of the patio chairs.

"Hi, Allie," Sophie greeted her. "We brought lunch: chicken and carnitas burritos, with a side of chips and guacamole."

"This is my girlfriend, Lizzie," John stated, introducing Allie to Lizzie. The glasses and side ponytails made Lizzie look a little nerdy in a cute sort of way. When she let her hair down and removed the glasses, the nerdiness would disappear and the cuteness would be enhanced. "Her last name is Abboud, which means 'a booty' in Arabic," he said as he poked her butt. Lizzie rolled her eyes at that.

"Last summer, her family went to the beach to dig for buried treasure. They were hoping to find a pirate's *booty*."

"Ugh. Stop," Lizzie groaned.

"When she was a baby, she pulled off her sock, and her mother said, 'Look, there's *a bootie* on the floor.'"

"Are you done now?" she asked.

"Yeah, until I can think of more."

Allie tried to stifle a laugh, making it come out as sort of a muted snort.

"Don't encourage him," Lizzie admonished.

"Sorry, I got caught up in the moment."

"It's nice to meet you." Lizzie turned to John. "You didn't tell me she's pretty."

"Yeah, I'm not stupid."

They went into the house and John began preparing glasses of water while Emi pulled out plates and forks. Sophie took the food out of the bag. Lizzie set her bag down on the sofa.

"Can I get some Tylenol or something?" Allie asked Sophie. "I have a headache." She recognized the effect of the roofie.

Sophie found the bottle of ibuprofen in the pantry and handed it to her before sorting out the food.

"Allie, do you want chicken or carnitas?"

"What's carnitas?"

"Pulled pork."

"Chicken. I don't eat pork." Allie's response was informative.

"We'll keep that in mind for future meals," Sophie commented.

When Lizzie first saw Allie, she recognized a vague familiarity. Not as if she had met her before, but as if she bore a resemblance to someone else she knew. She couldn't quite put her finger on it at first. However, the pork comment triggered a memory. Lizzie finally realized that Allie looked similar to her cousin back in Lebanon.

She asked Allie a question in Arabic and Allie responded in Arabic, perhaps unconsciously.

Switching back to English while also switching the subject, Lizzie said, "I brought some clothes for you. John said you looked about my size. Maybe after lunch, you can go through them and see if there's anything you like."

"Oh. Can I check anything she doesn't want?" Emi asked.

"Sure. How about a fashion show for anything you think is worth keeping?"

"Go back a few sentences," Ty said. "What language was that? What did y'all say?"

"It's Arabic," Lizzie said. "She sort of looks like my cousin in Lebanon so I decided to give Arabic a try." Lizzie looked to Allie to see if she would answer the next question.

"I don't eat pork because my family is Muslim. That makes me officially Muslim, too, but I'm not religious. My parents are super religious, but I'm not. I guess the pork thing shouldn't matter to me, but it's a habit that's hard to break."

"Are you ready to tell us your whole story?" Ty asked.

"The food looks good," she deflected, taking a bite of her burrito.

* * *

"Allie, what're you gonna do when we're at school?" Emi asked.

"I don't know. I guess just hang out in the backyard like I did this morning."

"School's a lot longer than church. You're gonna get bored."

Ty overheard the conversation. Too much idle time would lead to boredom, laziness, and depression. Ty wanted to help Allie but felt restrained without knowing her identity. She couldn't go on forever without anything to do. To reenter society, she needed a job, and when the new school semester started, she needed to go back to school. However, without a social security number and a driver's license or some other government identification, her choices were limited. *Baby steps*, Ty told himself. *She needs baby steps.*

"Allie, do you like dogs?" Ty asked.

"Sure. I never had a dog, but sometimes I played with my friends' dogs."

"Let me introduce you to Bob Barker."

He took her to meet his parents and Bob Barker, their large Labrador Retriever nearly as big as Allie. Bob Barker ran to get a chew toy and brought it back to Allie, wagging his tail.

"What does he want?"

"He wants you to play with him," Ty's mother Amanda explained. "He also likes walks." She held out a leash. "Do you think you could take him?"

Chapter 4
Building trust

Monday, Allie watched TV shows on her phone, via the house wifi and the family's streaming service account, but she could only take so much of staring at a tiny screen. She realized the laziness and boredom would drive her crazy.

Tuesday, she started following Ty's proposed agenda of jogging, reading, and walking his parents' dog. After returning from dropping off the dog, she noticed a weed in the flower bed in front of the Jensen house. As she pulled it out, she saw another. A half-hour later, she had a pile of weeds lying on the front lawn. Another half-hour took care of the weeds in the back flower beds. She checked the garage for a trash can. Not finding it in the garage, she checked the area between the garage and the neighboring fence where the family stored the trailer. The trash can sat just inside the gate. After putting the weeds from the backyard into the trash can, she dragged it to the front yard to throw away the remaining weeds.

"What're you doing?" Emi called out as she walked up from the school bus stop.

"Throwing away a bunch of weeds."

"Weeds?"

"I got bored, so I pulled weeds."

* * *

When Emi came home on Wednesday, she found Allie sitting on the patio, shirtless in a pink bra, reading a Harry Potter book, and displaying adhesive bandages on her chin and right arm.

"What happened?" Emi asked at the sight. Her bandaged appearance would have been more alarming had she not been sitting calmly with the book.

"Bob Barker decided to take *me* for a walk." She started giggling. "He saw a squirrel and took off. I fell and he dragged me through someone's yard until he finally decided I'm too heavy to drag around. He apologized, though."

"How does a dog apologize?"

"He licked my face. Then Ms. Amanda bandaged me up."

"Are you okay now?"

"Yeah, but I got blood all over my shirt. I think I got it all washed out in the kitchen sink in the trailer. It's hanging on the tree to dry. I would've put on a clean shirt, but I'm banished from the house."

"Are you up for another walk? This time without Bob Barker."

"Do you promise not to chase squirrels?"

"I promise. Let me put my backpack in the house, then we can go."

Upon exiting the house, Emi saw that Allie was still shirtless. "You might want to put your shirt back on."

"Why? I'll just get it sweaty, and this looks like a swimsuit top."

"But it's still a bra. Maybe a sports bra would be okay, but that doesn't look like a sports bra. Besides, I thought Muslim women liked to keep covered up."

"Yeah, well, a good Muslim girl doesn't get paid for sex either. I'm not even sure if I'm still Muslim. I guess I am, but I haven't really believed that stuff for a long time."

Emi handed the shirt to Allie, who put it on.

"One part of me wants to know about your time… uh… during… uh…your time before you came here. And another part of me is afraid to find out. For now, let's just start walking and I'll tell you about the neighborhood. I can show you the tennis courts, the elementary school, and the spot where Sophie and Ty got engaged."

* * *

Thursday evening, Sophie brought a college study group over for a late-night study session and sleepover. One of the girls was new to the group and when the others told her that Ty could do Black girls' hair, she demanded a demonstration.

"Touching someone's hair is a very intimate thing," Ty said. "I only do it for family members."

"Oh, come on, Ty. Hairstylists all over the world touch people's hair."

"Well, it's intimate for me."

The girls started chanting, "Tyler, Tyler, Tyler".

That brought John, Emi, and Allie into the room to see what the noise was about.

"Fine." Ty looked at Sophie. "Dutch braided pigtail with a fluffy end?"

"Sure," Sophie responded. Without being asked, Emi left and returned with a rat tail comb and elastics.

Ty moved behind Sophie and separated her hair down the middle before proceeding to construct a Dutch braid with the right half of her hair. He used the elastic to tie off the braid, leaving several inches unbraided, which he teased into a fluffy ball.

"How's that?" he asked, looking at the college girls.

"Kind of basic and the edge hairs are sticking up," one of the classmates pointed out, referring to the short hairs around Sophie's forehead.

Ty leaned over and licked the edge hairs to stick them down, prompting laughter from the college girls and a cry of "eww" from Emi. He finished it with a kiss on Sophie's forehead.

"Done," he announced, although only the right half of Sophie's head had the new 'do. The left half still had her usual style of tight coils. The college girls gave him a B+ for his effort.

"What about the other side?" Sophie called out.

"I've still gotta clean the kitchen."

After that, they tried to keep the noise level down as a courtesy for the others in the house, especially after the bedtimes of the other residents.

* * *

Saturday morning, Sophie went to Allie's room to gather her dirty laundry to wash. The others were responsible for their own laundry, but Sophie hadn't conveyed that to Allie yet. She wanted to let her settle in a bit first.

"Morning, Allie. It's laundry day," Sophie stated. "I'll help you this time, but next week you'll be responsible for your own laundry." Sophie set the empty laundry basket on the floor. "Put anything in the basket that needs to be washed.

"Okay, sure."

Allie disappeared into the closet while Sophie pulled the comforter off the bed to gather the sheets.

"Towels, too," Sophie stated as Allie dropped her dirty clothes into the basket and Sophie dropped the loosely folded comforter onto the chair.

"Okay."

"Don't forget the hand towel by the sink," Sophie added as she picked up the pillow to remove the cover.

As Sophie removed the pillow from the cover, she noticed a knife lying on the bed, on the spot that had been hidden by the pillow. It was one of a set of knives that belonged in the kitchen.

Allie came out of the bathroom with an armload of towels and saw Sophie staring at the bed. Sophie turned slightly to look at Allie. Allie then noticed what Sophie had been staring at. She glanced at the knife, then locked eyes with Sophie.

Both girls opened their mouths as if to speak, but nothing came out. After a moment of awkward silence, Sophie picked up the knife and set it on the nightstand next to the teddy bear.

"Put the towels in the basket," she directed upon finding her voice. She began stripping the sheets from the bed. After dropping the wad of sheets into the basket on top of the towels, she glanced at the knife on the nightstand, then looked at Allie. "Should we be afraid of you?"

"No," Allie responded softly.

Sophie picked up the laundry basket and walked out of the room. The knife remained on the nightstand.

On her way to the utility room with the laundry basket, she passed Ty in the living room.

"Come with me," she ordered quietly in passing.

Once in the laundry room, and out of earshot of the other family members, she told Ty what she'd found.

"And you left it there?"

"Yes."

"Why?"

"I didn't know what to do."

"How long has she had it?"

"I don't know. It could have been all week. We have several knives, and if one's missing, I just assume it's in the dishwasher. Do you think she's planning something?"

43

"Now you're the paranoid one."

* * *

In the afternoon, Allie heard the sound of a drill coming from Emi's room. She walked from her room through the bathroom to see what Emi was doing. Instead of Emi, she found Ty drilling a hole into the doorframe of the door between Emi's sink area and the bathroom.

Ty noticed her and looked up. "Hey. Sorry about the noise."

"What're you doing?"

"Installing a sliding lock."

"Oh." She didn't need to ask why.

"I'll put one on your door next."

She went back to her room without further discussion.

Allie sat on the edge of the sheetless bed and looked at the knife on the nightstand. She opened the drawer of the nightstand and used two fingers to slowly push the knife towards the edge of the top surface until it fell into the drawer. She closed the drawer, picked up the teddy bear, and held it to her chest.

That night, Allie noticed that Emi had closed her bathroom door for the first time since she had arrived.

* * *

She was running. The streetlamps cast an eerie glow on the debris scattered along the gutters. She could hear the steps of the men chasing her. She had a head start before they realized she had escaped, but they had more stamina. Her lungs cried out for air. But she continued running. Behind her, a deep voice called out, "You can't get away!" Ahead she saw a light from a building. An open doorway. People moving about inside. She ran for the doorway. As she neared, the door closed. She pounded on it with both fists, but it remained closed. She turned around to face her pursuers, back against the door, and slid down to the pavement. She drew her knees to her chin and lowered her head, sobbing. The first man to reach her grabbed her hair and yanked her head up while the other man delivered a blow to her face, open-handed so the bruises would heal faster.

* * *

On Sunday, Allie agreed to go to church with the family. Not that she became interested in church, but she didn't want to be alone, and she looked forward to dining out with them afterward. At their church, they had the group worship service first, followed by separate Bible study classes. Sophie and Ty went to a newlywed class and John and Emi each went to a youth class for their grade level. When the family went to their Bible study classes, Allie sat in the foyer and read one of the Harry Potter books. She wasn't the only one waiting. A few other teens also preferred the foyer to Bible study.

For Allie, the week had been slightly boring and delightfully normal.

* * *

Allie's second week with the Jensen/Butler family was similar to the first, without the dog walking injuries. No one popped pills, no one got drunk, no one forced others to have sex, and no one pretended to be a friend while leading her into a life of misery. As far as she could tell, they were helping each other succeed in school, to succeed in life. Afternoon walks with Emi became the routine. Emi said she needed the exercise and that the walks were also a good break between school and homework.

Thursday evening, the family hosted another college study group. The college girls went to the upstairs den, and John and Emi went to their own rooms, leaving Allie to help Ty clean up the kitchen.

"My name is Alia Khalifi. I'm from St. Louis."

Ty turned off the kitchen faucet and gave her his full attention.

"My parents are very religious, but not me. I was the rebellious one. The religious stuff just didn't make sense to me. My mother and sister and I would wear a *hijab* when we left the house, but I'd take mine off at school. I didn't get why we had to wear long sleeves and long pants in the summer when my non-Muslim friends could wear shorts and T-shirts. Even some of the other Muslim girls got to wear those, but not in my family.

"One time when I was at a friend's house, and she let me try on one of her summer dresses, the kind that didn't have sleeves and came down to about here," she drew an imaginary line across her thigh to indicate the length. "Not sexy, just

46

fashionable. I remember looking in the mirror and thinking I looked cute. And normal. Sorry, that's not relevant to why I'm here."

"Maybe it is."

"I left home about a year ago. I was sixteen. My father planned an arranged marriage for me. Not right away, but sometime after I became an adult. It was with a guy from Syria who I met once, a friend of a cousin. My father had already arranged a marriage for my older sister, but she's the obedient and submissive one and would do anything my parents said. I couldn't stand the idea of marrying someone I barely knew and didn't love, and came from a different country, a different culture. My parents still think of themselves as Syrian. I'm American. I think the guy's family planned to pay my father a lot of money for me, but I'm not sure. My father sometimes talked about having enough money to open a business after I was married off.

"I had a non-Muslim boyfriend, which pissed off my father. The guy was kind of nice and I liked being with him, but I think I was kind of using him to get back at my father. For the guy, I was an easy lay, but I was being easy so I'd be too messed up to marry. I sort of let it slip to my parents that I wasn't a virgin anymore."

"Did your dad call off the marriage?"

"Well, it *really* pissed him off. He gave me a beating for that because I dishonored the family. I had to sleep on my stomach for a week. Anyway, the answer to your question is 'no', the marriage was still on. He commented that it would take him longer to open his business, so I assume that meant he wouldn't get as much money from the Syrian guy's family.

"I complained about my situation on Instagram and I got sympathy from a lot of people. This guy I didn't know DM'd me. He said his name was Doug, but his friends called him Bulldog. That's what I get for not making it private, but I kind of wanted the world to know about my problem. Anyway, Doug and I DM'd each other for a few days. He was very sympathetic and he eventually said he could help me. I packed some things in a bag and went to the mall to meet him.

"He was good looking and seemed nice, like he had this vibe or aura or whatever you call it that gave me the feeling that I could trust him. The next few days with him were so good. It was kind of scary to leave like I did, but he made me feel okay about it. He encouraged me, gave me compliments, and made me feel special. The sex was great. He brought me to Houston. I felt like he was my only friend, but things started getting weird." She looked at the floor.

"He got me drunk and then made me have sex with his friends. I felt dirty after that, but he would praise me, buy me gifts, make it seem like it was normal. He said things like 'They're like my brothers. We're all part of a family. I love you so much.' He somehow made me believe that, like, I wanted it. He could also change from really nice to mean. It was some kind of psychological mind game, but I didn't figure it out for a long time. He made me feel worthless unless I did what he wanted. From there it became full-on prostitution."

"He was grooming you for the business."

"Yeah. I didn't even see the manipulation for what it was. Only after other girls were brought in and I saw it happening to them… that's when I realized what happened to me and I started planning to escape."

Ty couldn't tell for sure if she had finished her story or had more to go. After an awkward silence, he finally said, "I'm so sorry that happened to you. Are you sure you don't want to go to the police?"

"Are you kidding? They'll send me back to my father. Do you remember the dad in Dallas who killed his own daughters a few years ago because they dated non-Muslims? That'll be me if I get sent back."

"Thank you for trusting me. We'll figure out what to do."

Only when he reached for a notepad did Ty realize he had unconsciously balled up his fists. He forced his hands to relax, grabbed the notepad and a pen, and motioned for Allie – Alia – to join him at the table.

"Didn't you say your birthday is in January?"

"Yeah, January third."

"After you turn eighteen, they can't send you back to your parents. We just need to come up with a plan in the meantime. I don't want to lecture you, but you need to get back to school. I dropped out after my sophomore year and people treated me like a loser until I finally went back and got my diploma. So I think you should go back to school and graduate. I went to the community college to get my GED, but you're still high school age. Our school district has a high school that specializes in getting kids caught up after they missed a lot of school. And it's free."

"Good, because I don't have any money. I don't even have a bank account. I had a couple of thousand dollars back at the house, but we weren't allowed to have money with us when we were working. They said it was so we wouldn't get robbed, but I think it was really to keep us from running away. I left it all behind."

"We've already agreed to help you as much as we can. The school will be free and we're gonna pay for your basic necessities, but I thought you might be happier if you had your own source of income, even a part-time job. A legal one, that doesn't involve sex. It would give you some feeling of independence."

"What do I do?"

"Do you have a driver's license?"

"I had one in Missouri, but I lost it when I came here. I think Bulldog took it."

"What about your social security number? Do you know it?"

"No."

"Okay. We need to figure out how to get those without involving your parents because you'll need them to open a bank account, enroll in school and get a job."

Later that evening, Ty did a brief search on the internet for Alia Khalifi and found a short news article from over a year ago about a missing St. Louis girl. It corroborated her story.

Friday, they allowed her to stay in the house while the others were away at school and work.

Chapter 5
Lawn job

John walked into Alia's room, turned the desk chair toward the bed with Alia on it, and sat down.

"Ty said you might be looking for a job."

"Yeah, but I don't have a social security number, so I don't know how that's gonna work."

"I've got a proposition."

Alia looked at John curiously.

"I could use some help with my lawn business."

"What do you do?"

"I mow a bunch of lawns every week and get power washing projects here and there."

While his lawn business took up a lot of his time, it hadn't truly gotten to the point of being too much if he scheduled it right. The lawn season had only a few weeks left; by late November, the lawns stopped growing. He was being charitable.

"I'll pay you $50 per lawn for mowing and $100 for pressure washing a driveway and front walkways. You'll get sweaty and dirty, but it's money."

"Okay. Sure. Show me how."

Saturday morning, he showed her how to use the lawnmower, weed trimmer, and blower, which meant mostly learning the peculiarities of starting each piece of equipment. Although each device used gasoline and required pulling a rope to start, each had its own procedure of knob, lever, and button presses before pulling the rope. They practiced by mowing the Jensen lawn.

"What's the schedule?" Alia asked.

"I've got four lawns and a pressure wash job today. All are on other streets. And we're kind of running late now. I'll leave the ones on our street for you to do so you won't need the Escalade. You can do those during the week."

Alia helped John put a tarp on the cargo floor of the Cadillac Escalade and lift the mower and other equipment into the SUV. At the first house, John got her started with the lawnmower while he used the weed trimmer on the edges. They switched equipment for the second house. She watched him set up the pressure washer and start cleaning a driveway before she moved on to handle the lawn next door by herself. Upon completion, she took over the pressure washing job while John took the lawn equipment to another street for the last lawn of the day. Even in late October, the air was still hot and humid in the Houston area and the work generated a lot of sweat.

Although customers transferred money to John electronically, he paid Alia in cash from his secret stockpile in a lockbox chained to the desk in his room. His security predated Alia's arrival. It wasn't that he didn't trust his family members; he was paranoid of burglars. The immediate payment also gave Alia a certain feeling of independence, even though she still depended on the Jensen/Butler family for nearly everything.

"You've got to understand how nice it feels to be able to buy something, anything – even an ice cream from McDonald's – with your own money," Alia told John.

"How does this money compare to your… ah… what you did before?"

"Sex work?"

"Yeah."

"I got more for sex, but they always took a cut for their 'management fee' and charged for rent and food and other stuff."

"I bet it wasn't as sweaty as this."

"It was gross in other ways."

"Did you have any money left over?"

"Yeah. Some of the girls would blow it on drugs and alcohol, but I saved some."

"And you left it all behind, right?"

Alia just nodded.

"Well, just so you know, I'm only deducting the cost of gasoline. After all, we have to treat it like a business."

* * *

Sunday after church and lunch, John showed Alia the lawns on their street that needed mowing. She decided to do one on her own that day, while John was still available, in case she ran into any problems with the equipment and needed his help. She also decided that she needed a change of attire. After sweating buckets the day before, she borrowed a swimsuit top from Emi. She hoped that would keep her a bit cooler than the T-shirt she wore before.

When she completed half of a lawn, a gray Jeep pulled up into the driveway of the home whose lawn she was mowing. A red Camaro pulled in after it. An older teenaged boy stepped from each vehicle and gawked at the bikini-topped lawn girl as if they had never seen anything like it.

"Wow! She's a lot better to look at than the guy who mows our lawn," exclaimed Camaro guy. "Hey, can you mow my lawn, too?" he shouted, pointing at his crotch. His comments were really meant to make Jeep guy laugh. He hadn't intended for Alia to hear him over the noise of the mower, but quickly realized she had when she raised her left hand and extended the middle finger.

Jeep guy punched Camaro guy in the shoulder and shouted, "Shut up, dude. That was rude." Jeep guy shouted loud enough that it almost seemed that he wanted Alia to hear it as much as he wanted Camaro guy to hear it.

Alia had taken both hands off the mower's drive bar when she turned to flip the bird at Camaro guy. She'd forgotten that doing so would cause the engine to stop. The sudden quiet gave Jeep guy the chance to address her more civilly.

"I'm sorry for my rude friend." He seemed to search for something else to say. "You have beautiful eyes."

"My eyes? You can't even see my eyes from over there. Are you sure my eyes are what caught your attention?"

"Yes, your eyes. I'm sure they're beautiful."

She looked at him skeptically.

"I'm Caleb and this is my house. The rude guy's Andy. We – I've never seen you around here. I'm a freshman at A&M and I'm just back for the weekend."

"I'm Alia. I live over there with the Jensens," she said pointing to the house. Although the family unofficially recognized Ty Butler as the head of the household, the Jensen siblings actually owned the house and the neighbors still referred to it as the Jensen house. "And I'm John's assistant with his lawn business."

"You look hot."

Alia looked at him with raised eyebrows and tight lips.

"I mean, of course, you're hot."

Alia maintained her expression.

"I mean, it's a hot day. Let me get you some ice water."

Both guys ran into the house and Alia restarted the mower. Shortly, Caleb returned with a cup of ice water.

"Thank you," Alia said, taking the water and offering a slight smile.

* * *

After putting away the lawn equipment, Alia came into the house smiling curiously for someone who had just performed sweaty yard work.

"What are you smiling at?" Sophie inquired.

"I got two new lawn accounts," Alia explained.

"This is pretty late in the season to get new accounts," John commented.

"Maybe it's because you don't look as good as Alia in a bikini top," Sophie pointed out. Turning back to Alia, she said, "I'm guessing the people who came to you were men, not women?"

"Right," Alia responded, beaming. "And…" she held up a piece of paper.

"What's that?" John asked.

"A guy flirted with me in the middle of mowing and he gave me his number. First, he asked for my number, but my phone's not connected to cell service. His name is Caleb and he goes to A&M. Isn't that your school," she asked Sophie.

"No, he goes to Texas A&M and I go to Prairie View A&M. Maybe it's time to set up a cell service on your phone."

"I can pay for it with the lawn money."

"Let us worry about that. I'll check the available service plans. By tonight, you'll have a phone number."

"Maybe then I'll text Caleb my number."

"I'm glad you're making friends."

* * *

Monday night as Sophie unloaded the dishwasher and put away the utensils, she noticed the missing knife back in the drawer where it belonged.

Later that night, Alia noticed that Emi left her bathroom door open when she turned in for bed.

Chapter 6
The identity plan

"How's your gas station girl?" Dr. Ruth Odeku asked her niece, in her Nigerian accent. "She hasn't run away with the silverware yet?" Sophie had previously informed Aunt Ruth of the family's decision to take in Alia, for which Aunt Ruth scolded her for the risk.

"You know her name is Alia, not 'gas station girl'," Sophie corrected. "And she's more likely to organize the silverware than steal it." Sophie did not mention the missing knife. She didn't want to hear more of Aunt Ruth's scolding. "She's already organized the kitchen cabinets and the pantry. One morning I started a load of laundry before I left for school. When I got back that evening, I found she'd folded it and put it on my bed. We've also got her in the meal rotation now; she's cooking once a week for us."

"I'm glad she's found something constructive to do with her time."

Sophie filled Aunt Ruth in on Alia's involvement with John's lawn business and the attraction she received from the boy down the street.

"I don't mean to presume that the flirtation will advance to something more serious, but she should get tested for STDs. Bring her to the clinic this week."

"She doesn't have health insurance."

"Bring her in anyway. I'll work something out. There are programs for medical care for indigent youth."

"For what?"

"For children who are poor and homeless. You leave that part to me. Just bring her in. We have some openings next Wednesday."

"Okay. I'll check with her. I could bring her to school with me and take her to your clinic between classes."

* * *

Ty had spent the evenings at his computer researching how to best reestablish Alia's official identity without involving her parents. The key was in replacing her Missouri driver's license, which had to be done in person at a license office within the state.

One of the requirements for replacing a lost license was to provide another form of identification during the office visit. A certified birth certificate would do. Or a passport. She didn't have either. However, the website said certain less-official forms of identification are allowed, such as a school ID.

Another requirement was proof of residence. Examples of such proof were utility bills showing the name and address or an apartment lease agreement showing the name and address. Alia didn't have either. Ty sighed at the dilemma. *If there's a hurdle, you just have to jump higher*, he thought to himself.

Unfortunately, a new driver's license wouldn't be issued on the spot. It would be delivered by mail to the address listed on the license. Another dilemma. Another hurdle to jump. Ty formed a plan.

"We just need to get her a real driver's license with the identification number that she already had."

"For all your initial misgivings about Alia, you're really thinking hard about how to help her," Sophie chided her husband.

"Some people help by donating to a charity. We've got a real live person here who I can help directly. It kind of feels better than just giving money."

"So, what's the plan?"

"We need to get Alia to a license office in Missouri and that means a road trip. The closest office is in Joplin."

"How far is that?"

Ty pulled up the route in the mapping app on his phone.

"It'll be about a twelve-hour drive when you factor in stops for gas and meals. The Joplin office is open on Saturday mornings. That also means missing a school day."

"She's not in school yet. When do you plan on doing this?"

"I'm not talking about *her* missing school. I'm talking about *you* missing school."

"Are you thinking about this weekend?"

"The sooner the better. Even after getting the Missouri license, we have more steps to get her established here."

"I've got a class project that I have to work on each of the next two weekends. Don't you have some unused vacation days from work? You can take her."

"I thought all three of us would go. You'd trust me to go on an overnight trip alone with a girl who's used to sleeping with lots of men?"

"What about your mother? Can she go with you?"

"Good idea. I'll call her."

"But you know I trust you, even if your mom can't go. Before we were married, you had a chance to sleep with me and you didn't take it."

"I'd still feel uncomfortable on this trip without you."

"It'll be fine. Call your mom, but first tell me about the rest of your plan."

"Create a fake school ID, rent a mailbox from a mailbox store in Joplin, create a fake apartment lease agreement using the address of the mailbox, and go to the driver's license office."

* * *

Unlike a box at a real post office, a private mailbox will have a street address and a box number that looks much like an apartment number. Many such businesses allow the customer to call them to check if any mail had arrived and will even forward it to another address. Ty located a mailbox facility in Joplin. That would be their first destination to visit on Saturday before going to the driver's license office.

He found a sample apartment lease online and duplicated it on his computer. He filled in the mailbox company's street address, leaving the apartment number space blank for now. He would fill that in after securing the mailbox. Other fields included the names of the tenants, which he filled in with Alia's real parents, and the "other residents", in which he typed Alia's name. He made up the information for other fields. It just had to look real. He faked her parents' signatures.

The trickier workaround was creating a realistic school ID badge. He enlisted Emi's help to create a badge modeled after her own school badge. She printed it out on glossy photo paper. Emi watched as Ty glued the printout onto his old community college badge. It still didn't have the right feel of a real school ID badge, but he inserted the fake badge into a clear plastic sleeve attached to a lanyard. If the license office staff didn't take it out of the sleeve, it should look real enough for them to believe that Alia was who she said she was.

"Isn't this cheating?" Emi asked.

Ty winced as if pricked by a thorn.

"We're not trying to get something that Alia didn't already have. She's already in the Missouri driver's license database. All we're doing is bypassing the bureaucratic crap so they can find her record that's already there. Once they see her picture in their system, they'll know it's really her." Ty hoped that reasoning satisfied Emi. *It's not cheating. Much.*

* * *

Thursday afternoon, Dr. Odeku, also known as Aunt Ruth, called Alia to inform her of the test results. "You have two infections, chlamydia and gonorrhea. Both are treatable with antibiotics."

"Okay. Do I have to come back to the clinic?"

"I can send the prescription to the pharmacy that Sophie uses. It's the one right outside the neighborhood."

"That'd be good. I know where it is. I walked there the other day when I was bored."

"I'm also going to prescribe birth control pills. They won't help with STDs – condoms are better for that – but they'll help prevent a surprise. Whether you want to use them or not is up to you."

"I... uh...I don't think... um...I'm not going back to that lifestyle."

"Were you sexually active before then?"

"Um...yeah, but..." Her voice trailed off. "Okay. Thank you."

The thought of Caleb reminded her that there could be someone for her someday; if that someone could overlook a lot of baggage.

* * *

Thursday evening before Ty and Alia's road trip, Sophie visited Emi in her room to deliver laundry that had gotten mixed up with her own.

"It sounds like Alia's in the shower. Can you give these towels to her when she's done?"

"She leaves the door open, so you can go through and put them in the bathroom closet or just leave them by her sink."

Sophie peeked into the sink area to see that the door to the bath and toilet area was indeed wide open.

"Does she always leave it open?"

"Yeah. It's actually better this way. When that was your room, you always locked the bathroom door and then sometimes forgot to unlock it, so I'd have to bang on the door to get you to open it. Then you would yell at me for banging on the door."

"Sorry."

They heard the water stop and the shower curtain slide open.

"Now you can just hand the towels to her."

Sophie turned towards the bath area again and saw Alia toweling herself dry. Sophie turned back to Emi.

"She doesn't mind if you accidentally see her?" Sophie whispered.

"No. Sometimes we have full conversations while I'm at the sink and she's drying off or on the toilet."

"And you don't think that's weird?"

"At summer camp there was a girl like that in my cabin. She did everything in front of all of us. If anyone said anything to her about it, she'd just say 'we're all girls here'. What do they do in the dorms at college?"

"I wouldn't know since I never lived at school. This topic never came up."

"She should be done by now, so you can go through and give her the towels." Emi then raised her voice. "Hey Alia, Sophie's got fresh towels for you."

Sophie turned back to the bath area and saw Alia totally naked, hanging her damp towel on the rack. Alia looked over to see Sophie holding the towels with outstretched arms and an expression on her face that looked like a deer in the headlights.

"Oh, thanks. I need one for my hair," Alia said as she walked to Sophie to get the towels.

Back downstairs, Sophie found Ty brushing his teeth. "Change of plans. I'm coming with you."

* * *

In the early afternoon on Friday, the first weekend of November, Sophie and Alia were waiting for Ty to finish showering so they could hit the road. He had worked a half-day and arrived home at 12:30. They left the house 45 minutes later in Ty's truck. If they kept the stops to a minimum, they could make Tulsa by 10:00 pm and stay the night. Joplin was another two hours northeast of Tulsa.

Ty asked Alia to bring a book and read to them on the way to keep him awake. She chose *Harry Potter and the Prisoner of*

Azkaban. Alia sat in the front with Ty while Sophie took over the back seat with her computer and several reports, trying to do schoolwork and ignore the narrative.

"This isn't the first book, is it?" Ty asked as Alia started to read.

"This is book three. I read the first two over the last couple of weeks."

After dinner at a burger place in Durant, Oklahoma, Sophie and Alia switched places. Sophie had the task of finding suitable driving music on the radio. As she scrolled through the stations, she knew to avoid rap. Ty's response to that would be country, and although she didn't dislike country, it wasn't her first choice. She paused on a station that sounded like pop. A song she didn't recognize was just ending and she had to listen longer to see if the music met her taste.

Next up was a woman's sultry voice singing a slow ballad.

You are not hidden.
There's never been a moment
You were forgotten.
You are not hopeless,
Though you have been broken,
Your innocence stolen.

Sophie moved the radio tuner to find the next station when Alia shouted, "Go back!"

Upon going back, the sultry voice had gotten to the chorus.

I will
send out an army

to find you
in the middle of
the darkest night. It's true.
I will rescue you.

When the song finished, Alia said softly, "What's that song called?"

"The radio screen said it was 'Rescue' by Lauren Daigle," Sophie responded. "This must be a Christian station."

As they listened to the next song, Sophie and Ty heard sniffles coming from the back seat.

"Sounds like Alia may have allergies," Ty observed. "Pass her that box of tissues on the floor by your feet."

Sophie twisted around in her seat to pass the tissue box to Alia. Alia's eyes were closed tight and she had streams of tears running down her cheeks and dripping onto her legs.

"Alia, what's wrong?"

"I don't know," she squeaked out.

When the tears became audible sobs, Ty pulled the truck onto the shoulder of the highway and stopped.

"Are you okay?" he asked as Sophie opened her door and got out.

"Yes," Alia said between sobs.

Sophie opened the backdoor and slid onto the seat beside Alia. She put an arm around her.

"Was it the song?"

Alia nodded. "It means…," she started, trying to get her sobs under control. "For over a year," she took a big breath, "I felt forgotten… and hopeless." She sniffled. "And the song said…," sniffle, "…it said someone will send out an army to find the lost person. Me." After a few more sobs, "I'm sorry. I haven't cried like this in a long time."

"It's God. That's who sends out the army," Sophie clarified. She wrapped both arms around Alia and held her for several minutes while Ty looked on in silence, puzzled by such a strong reaction. The sobs eventually died down and Sophie picked up the box of tissues and set it in Alia's lap. Alia took several tissues to wipe her face and blow her nose.

"I'm okay," Alia eventually stated. "We can go on."

"How're you feeling?" Ty asked.

She looked at Sophie and reached down to clasp Sophie's hand before uttering her answer. "Safe."

They left the radio on that station until they drove out of broadcast range and the sound degraded into static.

* * *

On the ride from Tulsa to Joplin early Saturday morning, they rehearsed a back story if the license office staff asked.

"What happened to your old license?" Sophie asked, pretending to be someone at the license office.

"I recently moved from St. Louis and lost my license in the move. I need to change my address, too."

"Do you have proof of residency?"

"Yes, I have a copy of the apartment lease."

They expected the staff to focus only on the address listed in the document without further scrutiny.

"Do you have any other form of identification?"

"Only my high school ID badge. It's from my old school in St. Louis."

If asked, she would hand over the fake badge, still in the plastic sleeve with the lanyard attached. Hopefully, they would merely glance at it to see that the name and photo matched what they had in their system.

"I think you're set."

They made it to Joplin in time for the mailbox store to open up at nine o'clock. Thirty minutes later they had secured a mailbox under Alia's name to use for the pseudo apartment. Ty filled in the apartment number field on the fake lease document, trying carefully to make his handwriting look like the typewritten print. Upon completion, they used the copy machine at the mailbox office to make a copy of the lease, then to make a copy of the copy. The finished product looked like a document one would have for their own records while the original would have been held by the leasing company.

The next stop was the driver's license office, three and a half miles away. Alia would have to handle that part on her own.

* * *

The line at the license office was long. Alia waited forty-five minutes before she reached the clerk at the computer terminal.

She smiled politely as she stated her request for a replacement license with an address change.

As Ty predicted, they looked at her fake school ID badge but didn't examine it very carefully. In fact, the woman at the computer didn't even take the badge, she merely looked at it while Alia held it up. The woman put Alia's name into the computer and waited for the database to pull up her old information.

"Okay. Here you are. You're changing your address, too, right?"

"Yes. I lost my license in the move."

"Okay. Do you have proof of residence?"

"Yes. I have a copy of the lease agreement right here." Alia held up the document so the words "Lease Agreement" could be clearly seen at the top, and then flipped to the page that showed her name as an "other person" who would reside at the location.

"Shall I read off the address?" She offered to do that so the woman wouldn't need to examine the document closely. It looked like any other lease agreement, but Alia felt slight nausea as the clerk scrutinized it and imagined her finding some mistake that Ty might have made in creating it.

"Yes, thank you."

Alia flipped back to the address on the first page of the document and read off the address, including the fake apartment number.

"There is one other thing on the record," the clerk stated. "There's a note that says 'missing person'."

Alia froze. They hadn't planned for that.

"Um," she said, stalling. Thinking quickly, she said, "I think I know what that's about. A few months ago I got mad at my parents and went to stay with my cousin," she explained. She was also thinking of how to make it sound more plausible. "I told my sister where I was, but she was also mad at my parents and didn't tell them just so they would worry. When I finally showed back up at home, both of us got in big trouble. I thought the police in St. Louis cleared that up last year. Anyway, here I am. I'm not missing anymore." After that explanation, she held her breath.

The clerk looked around the room before turning to the clerk to her right. "Where's Carmine?"

"I just saw him walk to the back," the other clerk responded. "He was carrying a magazine, and you know what that means."

"Yeah, he'll be a while," Alia's clerk answered. She stared at her computer monitor for a moment and tapped a pen against her desk. Presently she looked at the doorway into the back room and at the crowd of people waiting to be served. She looked at the computer monitor and clicked the icon that would send an alert to law enforcement about the missing person along with the newly registered address. Momentarily, the nearby printer came alive and began printing a document. The clerk handed it to Alia.

"This is your temporary license. Use it until the new one comes in two to three weeks."

Thank god, Alia thought to herself as she slowly exhaled. She looked at the document and smiled, then frowned. She pulled out the apartment lease and compared the address.

"Oh, the address is wrong. It should start with '3', not '2'."

The clerk held out her hand for the temporary license. Alia handed the paper back and held up the lease, pointing to the address. The clerk clicked a few keys on her keyboard and another document emerged from the printer.

"Are we good now?"

"Yes," Alia replied after checking the address.

"Next!"

Alia emerged from the license office a few minutes later smiling broadly and waving the temporary license for Ty and Sophie to see from their position in the front seat of the truck, as if to say *mission accomplished!*

She planned to start calling the mailbox store every day in about ten days to check whether the license had arrived. When it did, she would direct the mailbox staff to forward it to the Jensen house by overnight carrier, for a fee, of course.

What the license clerk neglected to do was send a new alert to law enforcement after correcting the address. Later in the day, the store clerk at the Dollar General store wondered why police were asking about a missing girl living there. He assured them Alia Khalifi did not live or work at the store and he had never seen her before.

* * *

A couple of days later, Alia noticed a new photo hanging on the wall by the stairs. It was a photo of her in front of the Joplin license office, holding her temporary license.

Chapter 7

Sunday driving

They made it back home by ten at night, in time for a quick celebration with John and Emi before going to bed. A round trip to Missouri in two days was a lot of driving in a short amount of time. Yet, despite the exhausting drive, the family made it to church Sunday morning, including Alia.

Once again Alia went with the family to the worship service but waited in the foyer while they went to their respective Bible study classes. Worship was a diversion from her weekly boring activities and even proved to be somewhat interesting, from an outsider's point of view. However, she still did not feel ready to go to a Bible study class. She could be anonymous among the hundreds of congregants in the worship service, but a Bible study class was more intimate; she wouldn't be able to hide in the back. So she waited in the foyer along with other teens and read one of the Harry Potter books.

That is, until a woman came in and frantically asked for volunteers to help with the toddler class. She approached each teen and explained the situation that two other volunteer teachers had called in sick and they desperately needed at least one person for "crowd control". The volunteer wouldn't have to change diapers, just hand out juice and cookies and play with the kids, she explained. Each teen declined with some excuse or another, or simply walked away to another part of the building.

Alia felt cornered. She didn't have a ready excuse and the woman looked somewhat desperate and harried. Alia told herself that helping with toddlers wouldn't be a religious commitment. It was like helping at a daycare. She went with Mrs. Cortez to the toddler class.

"Thank goodness you're back," exclaimed the lone teacher. "This one keeps trying to kiss that one," she said, pointing at two youngsters. "And John Paul keeps trying to put the toy cars in his mouth."

"Well, we have a new helper," Mrs. Cortez said, introducing Alia to Anabel Kennedy.

"Could you keep the kissing kiddo occupied while I wipe down the toy cars?" Mrs. Cortez asked Alia.

Alia helped with crowd control during snack time and participated in a few rounds of the "Head, Shoulders, Knees and Toes" song, which required pointing to your own body parts while singing the names of those body parts. When it came to singing specifically Christian or Bible songs, she merely listened and kept the kids from wandering off. As the parents started arriving to retrieve their children, several of the toddlers gave her hugs before leaving with mommy or daddy.

As soon as the number of children dwindled to a number that Mrs. Cortez and Anabel could handle, Alia excused herself to return to the foyer where her friends would be expecting to find her. Mrs. Cortez asked if she could help again next week. Again, without a reasonable excuse to turn her down, Alia agreed to help. *It wasn't bad; it was kind of fun, actually.* It gave her something to do while waiting for the others, and the children didn't ask where she went to school or why she didn't go to a Bible class.

"How did you get roped into helping with toddlers?" Ty asked.

"Mrs. Cortez came out looking for helpers and I didn't have anywhere to hide."

As Ty laughed, John asked, "How was it?"

"I volunteered to help again next week."

* * *

That afternoon, while Sophie caught up on schoolwork, Alia asked Ty to help her practice driving. Since she was still a minor, the state of Texas required her to take a road test to get a Texas driver's license. If she could have held out a few more weeks until she turned eighteen, the road test would have been waived. However, she needed the Texas license before then to register for school, to prove she resided in Texas. It has been almost a year since she had been behind the wheel, and she knew that she would be rusty at it. Besides, Ty had already told her she could use his truck for the test and she had never driven a vehicle that large. She wasn't merely rusty, she was more than rusty.

"You haven't had enough car time for the weekend?" Ty teased.

"I've had enough riding time; now I need driving time," she responded. "You can just sit back and relax."

Not sure what her driving skills were like, Ty pulled the truck onto the street himself. He didn't trust her to back out of the driveway until he'd seen her forward driving ability.

She got into the driver's seat and adjusted it, adjusted the mirrors, and began adjusting the radio.

"Maybe you shouldn't get distracted with the radio until you get some practice driving around the neighborhood."

"I want to show you: I found a station that plays music like the one in Oklahoma. I'll turn down the volume for now."

She put the vehicle in gear and began slowly pulling away. Trying to compensate for the slow speed, she pushed the accelerator harder sending the truck leaping forward, just as she needed to make a curve to the left. She took the curve too fast, caressing the curb rather than the center of the lane. Being that close, the right side mirror collided with a mailbox, putting a big dent in the box.

"Sorry!" Alia exclaimed.

"You'll need to say that to the people at that house. It looks like they're coming to check it out."

With a heavy sigh, Alia stopped the truck and put it into park. With another heavy sigh, she opened the door and climbed out to face the man who had come out from the house. Ty got out as well, checking the condition of the side mirror and the mailbox. As Alia went to talk to the owner, Ty attempted to bend the mailbox back into its intended shape. He succeeded in getting the mailbox door to open and close, but the dent was still noticeable. Alia smiled as she returned to the truck.

"How can you be smiling?" Ty asked.

"I made a deal with him. I offered to power wash the driveway for free and he took me up on it. So we're good."

"So, you're smiling because he wasn't mad?"

"That too, but I'm really smiling because I think if I do a good job with his driveway, others might see it and give me business. So it's like getting advertising while paying off the mailbox damage."

"Thinking like a true businesswoman. Are we done with the driving practice?"

"No, we've only gone a block."

Her old driving skills came back to her as she figured out the necessary pressure to apply to the pedals to get the desired amount of accelerating and braking. After driving around the neighborhood for a few minutes, she headed out to a major road.

"Are you sure about this?" Ty asked. He had been gripping the handle above the passenger door and instinctively pushing his right foot against the floor as they approached stop signs and cross-traffic. "I was more relaxed when I was driving."

"I've gotten better. The last few streets were fine."

At the intersection to the main road, she properly timed the gap in the traffic and made a right into the flow without incident. After a mile, she did a U-turn and headed back, but made a right turn at a stoplight onto another major road. Ty began to relax as her handling became smoother. Apparently, her old driving experience really was coming back to her.

"Since you've gone this far, you might as well hit the freeway out of town. Let's go get banana pudding at the Buc-ee's in Waller."

"What's that?"

"What? Buc-ee's or banana pudding or Waller?"

"I know what banana pudding is and I assume Waller is a neighborhood or town. What's a Buc-ee's?

"You lived in Texas for the past year and never heard of Buc-ee's?"

"They didn't let me out much."

"Buc-ee's is a huge gas station with a combination convenience store, gift shop, and restaurant. Oh, and super clean restrooms."

"Okay. Whatever. Point the way."

Once they were on the freeway, she turned up the radio a bit to better hear the music. It would take another fifteen minutes or so to get to Waller.

As they waited in line for the banana pudding – enough for the whole family – Alia asked a question that had been on her mind. "What happened to John and Emi's parents?"

"Their parents died in a car accident about three years ago. Sophie and I have been looking after them since then."

"I know you guys just got married this year. Were you dating all that time?"

"No. We only started dating during the summer of last year. I lived in the trailer behind the garage and started off doing yardwork and basic handyman stuff for them after their parents died. Then I started driving Emi and John to their activities and helping with meals. Sophie was still in high school and I was taking GED classes at Lone Star College. Anyway, we started dating after we graduated."

"Wow! You started dating in the summer and got married the next spring? That was fast!"

"Yep. Our engagement was less than three months. We already knew everything about each other. Sophie pushed for the early wedding date. We meant it to be a small private ceremony, but word leaked out. Sophie's grandparents from Nigeria surprised us when they showed up."

They finally made it through the checkout line with a bag containing five cups of banana pudding and a Buc-ee's T-shirt, Ty's gift to Alia.

"You guys make a really cute couple. It seems like you've been together for a long time," Alia continued the earlier conversation as she removed her shirt in the parking lot next to the truck and replaced it with the Buc-ee's shirt.

Ty quickly turned his head away, surprised at her boldness. *Her personality is introverted but she's certainly not shy about her body.*

"You can look now, Mr. Prude."

"Most girls don't change clothes in public."

"Sorry. I kind of forgot what's normal."

Not knowing how to respond, he decided to resume the earlier conversation. "Me and the Jensens have acted as a family for a while. Meals together, vacations together, and all that. Did they tell you they adopted me?"

"How old are you?" Alia asked.

"Twenty-nine," he smiled at her confusion. "And Sophie's twenty."

"I didn't know you were that old. How could they adopt you?"

"It wasn't official, but it was two years ago. Then I adopted John and Emi back a few months ago. So we really adopted each other."

When they got home, Sophie greeted them at the door. Ty held up the containers of banana pudding for her to see.

"Oh, I'm glad you got my text. I wasn't sure since you didn't respond."

"What text?"

"When you were gone so long, I checked the tracking app and saw you were at Buc-ee's. I texted you to get banana pudding."

"You two really do know each other!" Alia exclaimed.

* * *

She couldn't see the creatures pursuing her, but their screeching roars announced their presence. She didn't know if the sounds were meant to intimidate her or to signal the other beasts of some sort of plan. There were at least two, maybe three. She ran. Between the outcroppings of rock in the dark desert wilderness, she saw a light. She pressed on, surprised that the creatures hadn't caught up to her yet. The light came from an open doorway in an adobe house. She heard the roars again. Maybe they were closer than she thought. She picked up speed for the last few yards to the doorway. She saw a person inside. The person was obscured in shadows, but the waving was unmistakable. It was a signal to come on, to come in. She leaped across the threshold just as the creatures arrived at the small house. The owner of the house pulled her inside and slammed the door behind her. As her eyes adjusted to the light, she saw the shadowy figure part and became two people. The shorter one, a young woman, held out a teddy bear. "For you."

Chapter 8
Mid-November Batman

It was John's birthday and Alia wanted to get him something. She briefly thought about the one thing that she already had, that men wanted, and that men found valuable enough to pay for. It wouldn't cost her anything to give him that as a gift, but it might be disrespectful to his girlfriend Lizzie, whom she liked. She brought up the subject of a birthday gift with Lizzie.

"You've got to be kidding," Lizzie stated in shock at Alia's proposed gift. "Uh…I'm fine with you giving John a gift for his birthday, but definitely not the 'free' one you have in mind. If he's gonna be dreaming about a girl, I want it to be me. Come on, I'll take you shopping for something more… ah… appropriate."

On the way to the mall, Lizzie spoke up. "I know you've lived a very different life from the rest of us over the past year. I can't imagine all the nasty stuff you had to go through, but I can guess that some of the things you had to do may have messed up your sense of …," she searched for the right term;

"…your sense of what's normal. Such as, normal girls don't sleep with another girl's boyfriend as a birthday present."

"I'm sorry. I should know that's not right. A year and a half ago, I would never ever have thought of doing that." After a couple of seconds of silence, she continued, "I wouldn't blame you if you'd slapped me. Please don't tell John. Or Sophie and Ty. I don't want them to have doubts about helping me."

"It's fine. It's just between us." After driving another block in silence, Lizzie asked, "Do you think of John as more than a friend?"

"If you're asking if I have a romantic interest in him, the answer is 'no', but he *is* more than a friend. He rescued me from the gas station, took me to a safe place, and gave me some of his lawn accounts so I could earn money."

After a couple of hours at the mall, with several side trips to look at clothes or other things that had nothing to do with John, Lizzie left with a bottle of cologne and Alia with a custom printed T-shirt with the phrase "Rescue Hero" and an action figure of Rocky Canyon, a character from the Rescue Heroes cartoon series. *John may be Lizzie's boyfriend, but he's* my *rescue hero.*

On the way back home, they passed a row of shops that had a small pickup truck parked facing the street with a "for sale" sign on it. $1,200.

"Can you stop there to check that out," Alia said, pointing.

"You're not seriously thinking of buying that, are you? It looks like they need to take it to the junkyard."

"I don't have much money, but maybe in a few months I could afford something like this."

The current subject was old, had paint chipped off of the roof and hood; was missing the tailgate; the passenger door and front fender were black, whereas the rest of the truck was dark green; and one wheel didn't match the others. A note on the window said it had 220,000 miles on it.

"I think I saw this truck here a few weeks ago. I can see why no one wants it," Lizzie stated.

At $1,200, it was still out of Alia's price range, but it set her expectations. She would need a lot more money for even a crappy car.

* * *

After dinner, John opened his presents. He immediately stripped off his shirt and put on Alia's Rescue Hero shirt. Lizzie opened the bottle of cologne and dabbed some on his face. She needed to show him the correct amount so he wouldn't overdo it.

When he thanked Alia for the shirt and action figure, she kissed him on the cheek. Lizzie looked at her and shook her finger in rebuke. "Watch it."

John then thanked Lizzie for the cologne. She wrapped her arms around his neck and kissed him fully on the lips, prompting laughter from Alia and the others.

"I have one more gift for you," Lizzie proclaimed as she held out a yellow gift bag with blue tissue paper protruding from the top.

John took the bag and removed the tissue paper to see yellow fabric. "Is this what I think it is?" he asked as he pulled out a yellow T-shirt with a black Batman bat symbol on the front.

The family began laughing.

"Are you wearing your panties right now?" John asked Lizzie.

Alia wondered what that meant. *Lizzie doesn't seem like the kind of girl to go commando. And why would a T-shirt prompt a question of her underwear?*

"I sure am. Just for this occasion. But you'll just have to trust me. No more attempts to rip my pants off."

That prompted more laughter from the family.

"That was an accident!" John exclaimed indignantly.

"Are you gonna explain what's so funny?" Alia asked to no one in particular.

"We were having a karaoke party here last spring and, right in front of everyone, John ripped my shorts off. And everyone saw I was wearing Batman undies."

"I did not rip your shorts off," John complained. "She was about to step on someone's toe and I grabbed her by the back pocket of her shorts to pull her back. I was trying to prevent an accident. And I only pulled off the pocket."

"But my shorts did rip and everyone saw my underwear."

"Yeah, especially after you pulled down your shorts and wiggled your yellow Batman butt at them."

Emi chimed in, "That's when the boy Tony said Lizzie was giving the bat signal and the girl Toni said John must be Batman."

Alia reached out to Lizzie's skirt and lifted up the back. "Yep, she's wearing the Batman panties."

"Hey!" Lizzie quickly pushed Alia's hand away and smoothed down her skirt.

"At least the ripped shorts weren't as bad as what happened to Sophie at the stingray exhibit in Hawaii," Emi stated.

"Do not go there!" Sophie commanded.

"Well now I've got to hear it," Alia said.

Emi started the story and others weighed in. Last spring, after Ty and Sophie returned from their honeymoon, Aunt Ruth announced her engagement to Dr. Ayodeji "Ayo" Diya. He had proposed the same weekend as Ty and Sophie's wedding. A few weeks later Aunt Ruth told them that they each accepted jobs in Texas, partly to escape the cold New Jersey winters, partly to try living in an area of less density, and partly to be closer to her nieces and nephew. She also explained that she and Ayo wanted to get married before they moved in together in their new location. They would have a small wedding in Hawaii in August, followed by a large wedding after Christmas in Nigeria, where she and Ayo were from. She encouraged the Jensen/Butler family to join them in Hawaii.

"Oh, there's a picture of that wedding on the wall by the stairs. I didn't realize that was Hawaii."

"Yeah, it's hard to see the background in the photo with all of us blocking the view, but it was on a mountain overlooking the ocean," Emi explained before continuing to recount the story.

One of the many activities they experienced in O'ahu, besides the mountain top wedding, was a visit to Sea Life Park with its many exhibits of aquatic animals. As they mapped out the exhibits and performances to see at the park, they took note of the exhibit that allowed guests to feed stingrays. What they didn't realize before they got to the stingray exhibit was that it was an immersive experience. They had been to a stingray feeding at the aquarium on Galveston Bay where visitors stood next to a large waist-high tank and fed the stingrays in the tank.

The exhibit at Sea Life Park was something else entirely. Participants were to get into a pool with the stingrays. The rays could swim right up to the visitors like friendly aquatic alien housecats looking for a treat. The Jensen/Butler family was eager for the experience but hadn't planned on needing to get into waist-deep water. They weren't wearing swimsuits.

"Do we skip it or go in with our street clothes?" Sophie asked.

"Ayo and I aren't going in," Aunt Ruth announced. "But you're young, you should do it. We'll hold your belongings so they don't get wet."

After removing everything they didn't want to get wet — shoes, belts, wallets, phones, etc. — and placing them in their backpacks, which were then placed at Ruth's feet, they were ready to enter the pool.

"Hold on," Sophie said. She removed her outer shirt, a Hawaiian print she had purchased only the day before, leaving on a white tank top. Sophie normally wouldn't leave the house without a bra, but she forgot to pack enough to last the whole trip and thought she didn't need one today since she had the extra shirt. She forgot that fact when she removed her outer shirt. *This is Hawaii*, she reasoned a few minutes later. *Many women in the park are braless, so I won't stand out.*

Now that Sophie was ready, the whole family entered the pool. Park staff provided dead fish for the guests to feed to the stingrays and showed them how to hold the fish between the knuckles of their closed fists when feeding. They didn't want anyone's fingers to be mistaken for food.

Stingrays swarmed around the guests, expecting the treats they knew would be provided. A bold stingray startled Sophie when it nudged her thigh from behind. She took a wrong step and slipped, submerging to her neck before a staff member caught her and helped her back to her feet. Sophie was slightly embarrassed for the stumble in front of the crowd.

There were a few gasps from the spectators standing around the pool. Not for the stumble, but for what they saw when Sophie stood up. The other guests in the pool, her family included, turned around to see what caused the gasp. That's when they noticed that Sophie's white tank top had become semi-transparent, revealing her womanly form for all to see. Sophie looked around, confused at why everyone was looking at her.

"Miss," said one of the park staff. "You need to cover up."

When Sophie still didn't grasp the meaning of the staff member's statement, he said more specifically, "This is a family park. You need to cover yourself."

Ty quickly pulled Sophie to face him and away from the onlookers and called out to Ruth for Sophie's outer shirt.

"So you basically flashed the entire park," Alia exclaimed.

"Yeah," Ty affirmed. "If it was a wet T-shirt contest, she'd definitely have my vote; she looked amazing. Do you want to see the pics?"

"What?! You have pictures?!" Sophie exclaimed.

"I got Ruth to send me the video. Then I took stills from the video."

"Give me your phone!" she demanded.

"I'm just kidding. I don't have any pictures to show." Just as Sophie's expression changed to that of relief, Ty added, "They're just for me to admire."

Sophie grabbed his phone.

Chapter 9
Official

The Monday before Thanksgiving, Alia's Missouri driver's license arrived in the mail, forwarded by the mailbox shop in Joplin. That began a flurry of activity to more fully establish her identity. The next day John took her to the Social Security office after school to get her social security number and request a replacement card.

"Now I can get a real job," Alia said enthusiastically as they walked out of the social security office.

"You don't think mowing lawns is a real job?"

"Yeah, but the grass isn't growing much now. I need something for the winter. Several stores have signs for seasonal help."

At dinner, Alia announced to the family, "I want to start looking for jobs. Sophie, on your way to school, can you drop me off at that big shopping center with the Bullseye store?"

"Sure. How will you get home?"

"John can pick me up after school. That'll give me time to hit all the shops to apply for jobs. I can just eat lunch at one of the restaurants in the shopping center."

"I can do that," John said. "It solves the grandma problem, too."

"What grandma problem?"

"Grandma's coming tomorrow for Thanksgiving. She'll get here before we get home from school and we were wondering how to tell her about you."

"She doesn't know about me?"

"She's a little weird about our relationships and how we do things," Sophie explained. "She took a long time to accept Ty into the family even after she'd done a background investigation, asked people at church about him, and actually invited him to spend time with us. I don't know what she'd do if she came here, thinking no one's home and then found you here by yourself."

"What am I supposed to do? Go back to Ty's trailer?"

"No. We were planning to tell her tonight and brace ourselves for her reaction, but now we can introduce you in person when John brings you home. I think she'll be okay with you being here when we're here."

* * *

Later that night, Sophie logged into the website for the Texas Department of Public Safety and scheduled a late afternoon appointment for Alia to take the road test required for a Texas driver's license for the Tuesday after Thanksgiving. John would have to take her after he got home from school. She and John could switch cars that day so Alia could use her smaller Mazda for the driving test. She didn't think even she herself could parallel park the Cadillac Escalade and didn't want to put that burden on Alia. Sophie read through the license requirements and noted that they included proof of Texas residency. The proof could be something like a utility bill or apartment lease.

That is something we have experience in, Sophie thought. *What worked in Missouri should also work in Texas.*

As Ty had done for the Missouri license, Sophie drafted a lease agreement based on a template she found online. This time, they could use a real residential address. She listed their home address and noted in the lease that it was for one bedroom with a starting date of the date Alia first arrived at their house. She thought stating "zero" or "free" in the space for monthly rent would make the agreement look fake, so she gave it a rate of $30 a month. Very low, but it was only for a bedroom. She signed the document as landlord and called Alia over to sign it as lessee.

After signing the lease agreement, Alia disappeared into her room and reappeared with $60. She handed it to Sophie, saying, "This is for the first month and for the month that just started."

"Alia, the agreement is just for the driver's license office. We're not really charging you rent."

"I feel like I should pay something. You've been doing everything for me. Please take it."

"We'll just save it for you for later. Maybe something for Christmas."

"I like dresses," Alia said in a quiet voice.

"Is that a hint?"

Alia nodded.

* * *

When John arrived home with Alia after picking her up from her day of job searching, they found Grandma already in the kitchen, arranging pots and pans in preparation for the Thanksgiving meal. John introduced Alia as a friend staying with them while her parents were out of town. It was technically true, so he wasn't lying to Grandma. He then texted the explanation to the other members of the household so they would all be on the same page of the story.

The weekend before Thanksgiving, Caleb had texted Alia to remind her that he would be home from college for Thanksgiving and hoped they could meet up. She felt that with the receipt of her driver's license and social security number, she could get into normal life. These documents were significant for Alia and she would like to have shared her excitement over them with Caleb, but unless he understood her background, the significance would be lost on him. *I'm not ready to give him those details. I want him to see me as normal before I hit him with that.*

Before he left College Station, Caleb texted Alia an invitation to join him and a couple of friends for dinner and tapioca tea afterward. She was somewhat averse to hanging out with a group of strangers. One person was fine, maybe two, but having to make conversation with them while hiding her background seemed a bit stressful.

"Caleb asked me out to dinner tonight," she told John and Sophie that afternoon.

"That's great! Did you say yes?" Sophie asked.

"I said I was planning to have dinner with you guys and that I'd have to see if I could politely get out of it. I'm not good with small talk and I'm not ready to tell the world what I've been doing for the past year."

"Just steer the conversation back to them," Sophie said. "People like to talk about themselves."

"At some point, someone's gonna ask about me, and it'll be awkward if I just don't answer."

"Your father wanted money to open some kind of business, right?"

"Yes. A small specialty grocery store."

"Okay. Your parents sold your house in preparation for opening a store in the Houston area. They're traveling around to arrange additional financing. You came to stay with us – old family friends – until your parents get the money situation finalized and settled down in this area."

"Okay. Why am I not in school?"

"This all happened in the middle of a semester, and you thought it would be easiest to just wait until the start of a new semester. You plan to catch up with summer school."

"Yeah, that's sort of true anyway."

"Selective truth. If they ask about details of what your parents are doing, just say you don't know."

Alia texted Caleb that she could go.

Caleb picked her up in his Jeep with the top down. She was glad she'd worn a jacket and that the ride to the restaurant was short. She had worn her hair down and it blew all over her face during the drive. By the time they reached the restaurant, it was such a mess that she tied it back in a ponytail. So much for trying to look cute for a date.

She felt a little disappointed to find that one of the friends they were meeting was Andy the Camaro guy. He was obnoxious when they first met. The other friend was a girl. Maybe Andy would behave better in front of his date.

"Hey, it's the lawnmower girl! Still as hot as ever," Andy commented upon her arrival. Apparently, having a date didn't curb his obnoxiousness.

"What did I tell you, Shelby?" Andy said, poking his companion with his elbow.

"Sorry about my cousin," Shelby said. *Cousin.*

"You're dating your cousin?" Alia asked her.

"Eww, no! I'm just staying with him for Thanksgiving."

No wonder.

"She just likes seeing Caleb 'cause she thinks he's cute," Andy explained.

"Caleb is normal. I don't know why he hangs around with you," Shelby responded.

"Shelby goes to A&M, too, but she lives in Arkansas," Caleb explained. "Andy's fun. Always the life of the party, but Shelby keeps things real."

Alia noticed that Shelby spent more time trying to keep the conversation going with Caleb than with Andy. *Was that due to family issues with Andy or to interest in Caleb?* she wondered. Overall, the evening went well. Not magical, but better than expected. Until…

"I saw you have a tattoo on the back of your neck," Shelby pointed out. Alia had forgotten about the tattoo of the butterfly with the dollar sign as the torso since it adorned a part of her body she couldn't see. "What's the story with that?"

The tattoo was the mark that her manager – her pimp – required all the girls in his stable to get. It was his brand, his logo. She had to think fast.

"A group of us girls got tattoos. A butterfly is cute, and we liked to dress cute, but we also wanted to make money, so it has a dollar sign." Selective truth.

"It is cute," Shelby said.

"Thanks." She breathed a mental sigh of relief. "Do you guys have any tattoos?" she asked to steer the conversation back to them, as Sophie suggested.

"I'm thinking of getting one," Andy announced, to which Shelby raised her eyebrows.

"Since when?" Shelby asked.

"Since I realized girls like guys with tattoos. Hey, if she can get one, I can get one. I'm thinking of getting a lightning bolt on one of my biceps."

"You may want to lift some weights first to give the tattoo artist more to work with," Caleb kidded.

At the end of the evening, Caleb drove Alia back to their street and parked in his own driveway, then walked her back to the Jensen home. At the door of the Jensen home, Caleb hugged her before saying goodnight and walking back to his house. *Just a hug.* Alia wasn't sure if he had lost interest in her or if he just moved slowly in relationships. She hoped there would be another date.

After she was back in her bedroom, she received a text from Caleb.

Caleb:
Saturday night?

Alia:
Another group thing?

Just you and me.

Things were already looking better.

* * *

The Thanksgiving meal included Ty's parents, sister, Aunt Ruth, and her husband Ayo. Ayo showed up in a white cowboy hat and western boots, which brought chuckles from Ty and Sophie. Ayo and Aunt Ruth were both from Nigeria and had only moved to Texas from New Jersey a few months earlier.

"Hey, Ayo. I see you're trying to fit into the small-town Texas lifestyle," Ty observed.

"He's been trying to hit all the barbeque restaurants in the area, too. He thinks that will make him a real Texan," Ruth explained.

"If he can learn to slow cook his own barbeque and invite the neighbors for it, they just might accept him as a real Texan."

"I'll work on it," Ayo laughed. "When I bought these I wanted to take them back to Nigeria in December to show off my new culture, but the hat will be hard to pack."

"Maybe get a John Deere cap," Ty suggested jokingly. "Then you'll really fit into the rural life and it's easy to pack. In fact, the more beat up it is, the more authentic it looks."

Alia had previously met Ruth – Dr. Odeku – under rather awkward circumstances. *How can you have a normal conversation with someone who has examined your private areas? No getting to know each other. No foreplay. Just, "climb up on the table, and let's have a look."* It helped that Ruth wore regular clothes today and didn't look as much like a doctor, but still awkward, nonetheless. Alia, to overcome her own discomfort, decided to join the conversation so her thoughts of Dr. Ruth would be about family, not medical issues.

"Are you going to visit your family for Christmas?" Alia asked.

"Not just that. Ayo and I are having another wedding ceremony. This one will be much bigger," Ruth answered.

"Congratulations. I heard a little about the wedding in Hawaii."

"Yes, we had a small ceremony so we could start our new life in Texas as a married couple, but we have to bring it home to Nigeria or our families there will forever hold it against us," Ayo added.

"By the way, you are looking good. Healthy," Ruth noted.

Now we're back to medical issues, Alia thought. She forced a smile and replied, "Yes. Thank you for your help."

She paused to think of a way to steer the conversation in another direction. "I looked for jobs yesterday and John will take me to get my Texas driver's license next week."

"That's fantastic. We've been praying for you."

"Thanks." *Is it normal for a doctor to pray for her patients or was the prayer because of the situation in which I ended up living with her niece?* Alia wondered. *I guess prayer should be considered a good thing, even for doctors*, she decided. *No harm if it doesn't work and it's nice to know someone's thinking good thoughts for me.*

Grandma Jensen looked somewhat confused during the Thanksgiving meal. She referred to Alia as John's girlfriend. John tried to correct her, but she repeated the assertion later in the day. Sophie gave Ty a knowing look. She recalled the times before they started dating when people assumed they were a couple simply because they shopped for groceries together.

Alia wasn't sure whether she should play along in the role of girlfriend or try to correct Grandma. After lunch Grandma made everyone line up for photos by the fireplace. She took snapshots of various combinations: grandchildren individually, she and the grandchildren, then a group photo of those three with Ty, then Ruth and Ayo, then the Jensen siblings with

Ruth. Lastly, she called for a photo of John and his "girlfriend" Alia. They had given up on correcting Grandma by then and dutifully posed side-by-side in front of the fireplace.

"Come on, you two. Look like you like each other," Grandma called out. The others chuckled in amusement.

Alia turned to face John and pulled him around to face her, with their sides to the camera. She wrapped her arms around his neck, lifted one leg slightly off the floor, turned her face to the camera, and smiled sweetly.

"That's more like it," Grandma said as she snapped another photo.

"Emi, next year are we going to get a picture of you and a boyfriend?" Grandma inquired.

"Don't count on it," Emi replied.

"Are you gonna show that pic to Lizzie?" Emi asked John later.

"Are you crazy?" he replied emphatically. "And you better not tell her."

Emi pressed her lips together and made a motion with her hand, pretending to zip her mouth shut.

"Can I get a copy of the pic?" Alia asked John.

"As long as it's not for blackmail," he replied.

They finished off the Thanksgiving festivities with their custom of Christmas carols sung to the accompaniment of Sophie on the violin, John on the piano, and Ty on the guitar. The Butlers were used to the carols as they had been participants for the past three years. This marked the first time for Ruth, Ayo, and Alia. Alia wondered why she didn't know they could play. After all, she had been living with them for several weeks. The presence of a piano should have been a clue, but she hadn't seen anyone play it before. *They have their own little band here.*

After the small concert, Alia pulled the three siblings aside and said, "That was fun. You guys should do some love songs for your aunt's wedding."

"We're not going to the wedding. It's in Nigeria."

"I mean, record them here and send them to whoever's planning the wedding. Like a wedding gift from you to them."

The three looked at each other. John raised his eyebrows in a "what do you think" expression.

"One song," John said.

"Two. One for the bride and one for the groom," stated Emi. "I can sing the bride song and John can sing the groom song."

They looked at Sophie. "We have about a month to get it right," she said. "And, Alia, since you brought this up, what will you do?"

"I can help more around the house to give you time to practice?" she said in a questioning voice. "Oh. I know. I can bang on stuff."

"What does that mean," Emi asked.

"I think she means she'll be a percussionist," Sophie guessed.

"Yeah. Like we did for music class in elementary school. I can hit sticks together or shake a bottle of dried beans."

"Okay," Sophie agreed. "That's a good idea. Not just about Alia shaking beans, but I mean the whole idea of performing wedding songs for them. Since we can't be there, this is how we can participate. Emi, John, are you willing to put in the practice?"

"Yes," they both said at the same time.

"I'll tell Ty. We'll need him on guitar," Emi stated. "Not for singing," she added. John and Sophie laughed. They'd heard Ty sing.

* * *

The Thanksgiving photo of the whole family, including Alia, showed up on the stairway wall a few days later. The photo of John and Alia hung next to it. However, that photo disappeared by the end of the day.

Chapter 10
Date spying

Grandma returned to Dallas on Saturday. Sophie and Ty were able to move out of the upstairs den back to their own bedroom where Grandma had been staying.

That same morning, Alia received a call from the manager of Bullseye Home Essentials, one of the stores she had applied to. She asked if Alia could come in on Monday to fill out employment papers and start training. *This was definitely a good weekend.*

* * *

Alia had her second date with Caleb on Saturday evening. It was a movie and then coffee afterward to talk about the movie. This time it was just the two of them. She almost offered to pay her own way, but she liked the idea of a guy paying for her to have a good time, rather than paying her to give him a good time. After the goodbye hug on their previous date, she knew he wasn't after her for sex. Maybe next time she would pay. Caleb had given her the choice of a romantic comedy or an action flick. Romance seemed to her to be just as farfetched as explosions and car chases. She chose the action movie. At least you were less likely to be fooled into thinking the plot was something that could actually happen.

This time the roof of the Jeep was up and the doors were in place. A light rain had started earlier in the evening and Caleb met her at the door of the house with an umbrella in hand. He put one arm around her waist to keep her close under the umbrella as they walked to the car. At the touch, she glanced at him and smiled. *This feels good.*

In Alia's previous life in St. Louis, dating was done as a group activity. More like the dinner with Andy and his cousin. Then it seemed to jump from group dates to physical intimacy in one leap, bypassing any intermediate steps of one-on-one time in public. Alia wasn't sure if that was the high school way of doing things, or if it was due to her rebellion against her father short-cutting the process. She was eager to see how the intermediate steps played out.

* * *

That night John and Lizzie had their own date. Lizzie wanted to watch a romantic movie, but it was John's turn to pick the movie and he chose action. *Really, how many guys would choose a romcom on their own?* Lizzie thought. *Go into a movie theater playing an action movie and see how many guys are there by themselves or with their guy friends. Then go into a theater playing a romance movie and compare how many guys are there by themselves or with guy friends. Very few for the romance movie. Girls have a broader taste in movies than guys.*

She spotted Caleb and Alia settling into seats two rows in front of them and pointed it out to John.

"I'd invite them to sit with us if there was room," Lizzie stated. "Let's go say hi."

"No, let them have their private moment. I don't want them to think we're spying on them."

"That's why we should go say hi. So if they see us later, they'll know we weren't just spying."

The lights dimmed at that moment, saving John from further argument. It was apparent that Lizzie also gave up the effort when she raised the armrest separating their seats and grabbed John's arm, resting her head on his shoulder.

In the cinema, Alia leaned her body towards Caleb so that their shoulders touched. Caleb's arm was on the armrest between their seats. About twenty minutes into the movie, Caleb moved his hand palm up. Alia put her hand on his, palm down. He intertwined his fingers among hers and closed them. Alia felt a tingle throughout her body and her heartbeat sped up. She wondered if the tingling sensation was something only she could feel or if Caleb could tell that she had it.

She'd experienced a similar tingling before in the earliest days of being with Bulldog after running away. That was when he was trying to win her over and she fell for it. However, Caleb had no agenda as far as she could tell. She knew where he lived, knew where he went to school, and knew he seemed to take it slow with relationships, at least with her. This was a good tingling.

By the first few minutes of the movie, John had forgotten about Caleb and Alia. It was only when Lizzie elbowed him and pointed did he turn his attention back to them. Caleb and Alia were now holding hands and Lizzie thought it was noteworthy. John was also holding Lizzie's hand and he held up their clasped hands as if to point out they were doing it, too. So what?

When the movie was over John insisted they hang back and let Caleb and Alia leave first. He still didn't want to interrupt their date.

* * *

At the coffee shop, Alia let Caleb do most of the talking. She missed some of the parts of the movie as she lost herself in thought. The coffee talk filled in the gaps. She was thankful the conversation didn't turn to her past.

* * *

After the movie, John went to Lizzie's house to hang out for a while. Her parents allowed them in her bedroom only if they left the door open. That was fine with them. They chatted about the movie, FaceTimed with friends to see what they were up to, and looked up cat videos on YouTube. Neither of them had a cat. John left when Dr. Abboud came in to remind them of the time. Although no curfew had been discussed, Dr. Abboud's reminder indicated that one existed.

When John turned onto his street, he saw Caleb's Jeep parked in front of their house. John continued up the street and circled the cul de sac, stopping a few houses down and turning off his headlights. He wanted to give them a moment of privacy before pulling into the driveway.

Caleb walked Alia to the door of her house. The rain had stopped while they were in the movie, so the umbrella wasn't needed. That also freed up both of Caleb's hands for a hug. *Even if it's just a hug*, Alia thought, *it was still a good night*. With his arms around her, he pulled her in for a kiss. *This is a great night!* she amended.

John saw the kiss and said to himself, "Good for her." He was happy for her to have a healthy relationship after the bad year she'd had, but he also had an odd feeling inside. "Stop it," he continued the conversation with himself. "I have a girlfriend and now Alia has a boyfriend." After Caleb drove away, John turned the headlights back on and pulled up into the driveway.

Chapter 11
A Texas Life

After the Monday afternoon meeting with the manager of Bullseye, Alia was now officially employed. It was not full-time, but enough hours to keep her busy. She estimated she could pull in a few hundred dollars in December. Not enough to live on, but enough to pay for her own things and not have to rely on Ty and Sophie for everything, and maybe Christmas gifts. The employee discount would be helpful, too.

One thing that she hadn't counted on was the need for a bank account to deposit her salary into. She knew they wouldn't pay her in cash but hadn't really thought through the logistics of the payment process.

As John drove her back from the shopping center, Alia noticed a bank on the way. She already had a few hundred dollars from three weeks of lawn mowing and power washing. Her thoughts drifted to the upcoming driving test to get her Texas driver's license. She had to take the driving test because she was a minor. Adults didn't have that requirement. That thought brought her back to the bank situation. Would she be able to open an account on her own as a minor? She checked the bank website on her phone and saw that the service hours indicated the bank was already closed. She made a note to call tomorrow while waiting for John to take her to the driver's license office.

> Alia:
> I filled out employment papers today. I am officially a Bullseye employee. My first day is Wednesday

Caleb:
That's great. It's always good to have extra spending money

> Now I need to open a bank account

You don't have a bank account? Not even a savings account?

> I guess I'm just behind the times

Her new employer had wanted her to start Tuesday, but she explained she was already committed that day. She didn't tell them she was scheduled for the driving test and that the logistics of getting it took up pretty much her whole day. Wednesday afternoon would be her first shift. Everyone in the

Jensen family would be gone at that time. So Alia had two problems: how to get to and from work and how to open a bank account.

Just then, they passed an old man on a bicycle.

"I hate when bicycles take up a lane," John complained. "They go so slow."

* * *

Tuesday afternoon, Ty, Sophie, and Emi received a single-word text message from Alia. "Passed!" She was now on record as an official Texas resident with a driver's license. When John and Alia arrived home, the four teddy bears on the fireplace mantle had been joined by a fifth bear.

> Alia:
> Passed!

> Caleb:
> Congratulations!

He included a 'thumbs up' emoji. The app displayed balloons and confetti when she opened the message.

> Now I feel like I'm officially a
> Texan. I just need something
> to drive

> When the money starts
> rolling in, maybe you can buy
> a car

For now, I guess I'll be the
slow cyclist blocking traffic

Every day, she and Caleb found a reason to text each other.

* * *

Wednesday, Alia rode John's bike to Bullseye and Ty picked her up on his way home from work, putting the bike in the back of the truck. On the bike ride there, she had kept the new red shirt and black slacks of her uniform in a backpack to change into once at the store. She correctly assumed they would get dirty if she wore them on the bike ride. The legs of her jeans had little splatters of dirt all over them from riding through the occasional water puddles that pooled in the gutter.

* * *

Ty arranged to go into work late on Thursday so he could take Alia to register for school and open a bank account. They had been waiting for the driver's license to show proof of residency within the school district. If she had failed the driving test, the backup plan was to get a Texas identification card. Fortunately, that wasn't necessary.

The school noted that Alia was a minor and would need parental approval. However, since the first day of the spring semester was after her eighteenth birthday, the administrator was willing to waive the requirement. He could plan for her arrival, but wouldn't turn in the paperwork to the district until at least January 3rd.

Alia:
I'm registered for school now

Caleb:
Not sure if I should say great
or I'm sorry

My life has been messed up
for long enough. I look
forward to getting back to
normal

And school is normal

Okay, then Great!

You're looking forward to
school starting and I'm
looking forward to it ending

Ty signed on to Alia's new bank account as a cosigner. They planned to return in a month to close the account and have Alia open a new account without a cosigner. Both thought it ridiculous that the bank couldn't just remove a cosigner at the designated time, but the service desk described such an involved process to do so that the easiest method was to simply open a new account and close the old one. Even the bank manager agreed that was the most efficient method.

On the drive home, Ty brought up a sensitive subject. "You've got your identity back and you're about to turn eighteen. I think it's safe to go to the police about the sex trafficking ring. I doubt they would force you to go back to your parents now."

"Maybe, but going to the police won't do any good now."

"Why is that?"

"Everyone would've changed houses right after I left. That's the way it works. If they think there's a possibility of the police raiding the place, they move; and my running away would have made them move. I think Bulldog has a permanent place. He only stayed with us two or three nights a week."

"And you don't know his real name?"

"When we first met, he said his name was Doug Smith. But I know Smith isn't his real name. The other guys also used Smith and I know they're not related. I don't even know if 'Doug' was his real first name."

* * *

As Alia fell into a work routine with the department store, she still found time to take Bob Barker for daily walks. Sometimes it had to be in the morning, and sometimes in the afternoon, but she rarely missed a day. She made sure to not wear her Bullseye uniform for those walks because they were often messy. The walks always involved a few rounds of fetch and ended with cuddles on the Butler's front lawn. If Alia was pressed for time, she would shorten the walk, but keep the cuddles. As much as Ty's parents appreciated her effort with their dog, she wasn't doing it for them. She was doing it for the cuddles.

* * *

On Saturday, Alia watched Ty and John load up Ty's truck with tools for the church's senior volunteer work. It was a time when men and boys from the church formed teams to help elderly church members with handyman projects. This time the equipment included a portable table saw and pneumatic nail gun.

"I thought your handyman projects were about fixing shelves or changing lightbulbs and stuff. Do you always need this much equipment?"

"Not usually, but this time our team is repairing a fence, so I'll need to cut boards and nail them up."

"Is all this yours," she asked Ty, "or left from John's parents?"

"This is mine. I got most of it a few years ago when I bought an old house to renovate."

"So, you're good at fixing things?"

Ty laughed. "It depends. I can definitely fix a fence, though."

"Can I come?" she asked.

"Don't you have to work today?"

"Oh, yeah."

As they drove out, John commented to Ty, "Why didn't you tell her it was just for guys?"

"I wasn't prepared to get into a conversation about sexist stereotypes."

"I think she just wants to be part of something."

Alia watched them drive away. It was too early to get Bob Barker for his daily walk. She would wait for the dew to dry first.

Alia:
When are you coming home?

Caleb:
I'm still in finals. Be back
next weekend. Ask for Sat
nite off from work

Ok.
I'm looking forward to seeing
you again

* * *

Caleb came home from college a few days before Christmas. Alia put in a request at work to have off Saturday night. She already had a standing order to keep Sunday mornings free. A Sunday work schedule would have given her an excuse to avoid going to church with the family. After all, she didn't believe what they believed. She didn't believe anything. Nevertheless, she liked going to church. The music felt good. She sometimes found herself singing along without realizing it. The people looked happy as they greeted friends before and after the service and she liked helping with the toddlers. It was especially nice when they recognized her and looked glad to see her.

The Saturday date with Caleb again involved dinner, this time without his sidekick Andy. Alia walked to his house and met him in the driveway. He opened the passenger door of his Jeep and helped her in. This was their third date and she smiled at the chivalrous nature of that act. It seemed old-fashioned, but sometimes old-fashioned felt nice.

Although they had been texting each other since their last date after Thanksgiving, texting couldn't take the place of face-to-face conversation. Alia had several big life events over the past three weeks to share and Caleb had his experience with finals and opinions on the classes that just ended. Which class was boring, which was interesting, and which professors were full of themselves. Not to mention the parties that students had going into finals.

After dinner, they drove back to the neighborhood, parked in Caleb's driveway, and decided to take a walking tour of Christmas lights. As they walked, Caleb reached down and took her hand. *Is this the Hallmark movie moment when snow is supposed to start falling?* Alia thought to herself. After an hour of viewing the lights and visiting the Christmas tree at the community center – she commented to Caleb that she'd heard that was where Ty and Sophie proposed to each other – they arrived back at the Jensen house.

"I don't want this to end. Can we go to your house?" Alia asked.

"My parents are there and they're pretty nosy. We won't have much privacy. What about your house?"

"Same. Ty and Sophie are sort of like a mom and dad, maybe not as nosy, but Emi would be right there wanting to know everything." She thought a moment.

"Come with me." She grabbed his hand and pulled him up the driveway to the backyard, behind the garage, and to the travel trailer stored there. She almost told him it was the place where she was banished for the first two weeks with the Jensens, but remembered that Caleb didn't know her background and that would open up a whole new topic of conversation. She pulled out her key, unlocked the door, and turned on the lights.

"Hey, this place is cool," Caleb remarked, exploring the trailer. "Do y'all go camping a lot?"

"Not since I've been here. Ty used to live in it before they got married. We can have some privacy here. I just need to figure out how to start the heater."

"Where do people sleep?" Caleb asked after noticing only a dinette on one end and a sofa on the other.

"The sofa converts into a bed. Watch." She demonstrated the conversion. "The dinette also makes into a bed and that thing above the dinette folds down into another bed."

"That's cool. My family once rented an RV for a trip to Garner State Park. It was a lot of fun."

Alia removed her jacket and sat down on the edge of the bed. Caleb followed her example.

"I really enjoyed tonight," Alia said. "It's been a long time…"

Caleb leaned in and kissed her mid-sentence. Alia felt warm tingles throughout her body. When they parted, she leaned her head on his shoulder. She was going to say it had been a long time since she had felt close to a guy. Was that even true? The guys in her life had merely used her. Her first boyfriend just wanted sex, but she also used him to get back at her father. Her second "boyfriend" was merely pretending he liked her to lure her into the sex trade. Caleb was the first who didn't seem to have an underlying motive for the relationship. That just made her feel all the more warm and tingly.

She suddenly wrapped both arms around his neck and kissed him again. It was awkward sitting side-by-side on the edge of the bed with their torsos twisted towards each other. He pulled her sideways onto his lap and put his arms around her. Still kissing, he fumbled with the back of her shirt until he found the tail and put his hands on her back, under her shirt, skin to skin. Alia felt her tingling sensation intensify. Not really tingling, but warmth and pressure in her lower regions; and a feeling like she had an emptiness in her heart that begged to be filled.

"Wait," Alia said suddenly, interrupting her own moment.

Caleb, assuming he knew the cause of her interruption, reached into his back pocket and pulled out his wallet.

Whatever was the cause of Alia's break didn't involve a wallet and she froze, holding her breath. She was well experienced with men opening their wallets before an encounter with her. It was a past she didn't want to revisit and she wondered how Caleb knew about it.

Caleb opened his wallet and pulled out a condom packet. Alia exhaled and started breathing again. "My dad gave me a box when I started college and said I should always keep one with me."

The evening was getting late and Ty was ready to lock up the house, but Alia was still not home from her date with Caleb. They hadn't discussed when she might be back. She wasn't a child, and certainly not his child. However, Ty was still a bit concerned about her welfare. It was like the time he waited up for Sophie when she was late getting home from Homecoming. Of course, that was before they had even started dating, back when he was merely the household handyman/advisor, a position he had jokingly called "the butler". Ty remembered the tracking app he had installed on Alia's phone. They all had it and they were all able to track each other. *It's not spying*, he told himself. *It's for safety*.

He looked up the app and saw that it said she was home, although he knew she wasn't in the house. He went to the front door and looked out. He didn't see anything. Not even a car parked on the street in front of the house. He went out into the front yard and looked around, then headed to the driveway to walk around the side and to the back. Once in the backyard, he saw a faint glow coming from behind the garage and smiled to himself. *Clever girl; found some privacy.*

Standing beside the trailer, he called out, "Hey Alia, sorry to interrupt. Just wanted to say we're going to bed. I'll leave the back door unlocked for you. Please lock up when you come in, but no rush. Good night."

Busted! "Okay. Good night!" Alia responded.

"Good night, Caleb," Ty added.

"Uh, good night."

"I hope you have protection."

"We're good," Alia replied.

Caleb and Alia looked at each other.

"That was so embarrassing," Caleb exclaimed, lying back on the bed, feet dangling off the side. "At least it wasn't your parents. Or my parents."

Alia scooted off Caleb's lap and lay back on the bed, too, next to him, and started laughing. "We were so busted." She soon turned serious and pointed to the condom packet. "That's not why I stopped; although I do appreciate it."

She paused, trying to formulate her thoughts about what she wanted to say. She felt she was being unfair to move to a deeper relationship without opening herself up and revealing her past. She thought she knew enough about him, but she had been purposely withholding a significant part of herself from him.

"I haven't been open with you about myself. I really like you and I think you deserve to know more about me before we go further." She sat up.

"I like you, too, and I do want to know more about you. I doubt there's much you could have done to change my mind about you."

Alia proceeded to tell him the same story she had already told Ty and Sophie. Abusive father. Running away with a stranger she met on the internet. *That was pretty heavy*, Caleb acknowledged, but not enough to deter his affection. He picked up her hand and kissed it.

"It's okay. That's in the past."

"I haven't gotten to the worst yet." She explained how the internet stranger lured her into the sex trade and forced her to spend the better part of the past year as a prostitute.

"John found me and they're helping me get my life back together."

Caleb was no longer lying down. He was still holding her hand, but it was no longer at his mouth ready for another kiss. It was now in between them on the bed. Alia could see that his earlier passion had dimmed.

"That's a lot to take in." He was quiet for what seemed like minutes. "You've been hurt – abused – by a lot of men over the last few years. Even good relationships can sometimes hurt and I don't want to be another one to hurt you, even accidentally. I don't want to do any further damage." He was quiet again.

"I need to think about this," he said as he stood up. "I had a great time tonight, but it's late and my parents are probably wondering where I am. I'll call you." He walked out of the trailer.

123

Alia shivered from the cool air when Caleb opened the door. *He doesn't want to further damage me*, she reflected. *That's me: damaged.*

She wiped her tears before finally locking up the trailer and going to the house.

Chapter 12
Rahab

At church on Sunday, Alia felt self-conscious of her background. Ty, Sophie, and the others accepted her, but after Caleb walked out on their date, she had fresh doubts about her place. This was a religious place, with certain expectations for beliefs and behavior. If it was anything like the *masjid* her family attended, there would be quite a few people bothered by her presence.

If others knew what I told Caleb, would they want me around? Would they trust their children with me? It wasn't a new thought, but it became more prominent after Caleb's reaction.

"You've been a bit quieter than usual this morning. Are you okay?" Mrs. Cortez asked Alia while they prepared snacks for the toddlers.

"Sorry. I'm a little down, but I'll be alright."

Mrs. Cortez looked at her skeptically. "Spill it."

Alia looked around the classroom. The other volunteer was busy leading the children in a song session. "I met a guy and thought things were going well, but I've done some pretty bad things in my past and he couldn't handle it. I don't know if he's going to come back around or not. Now I just think about whether that stuff is going to haunt me forever. Like, am I just totally ruined?"

"I want you to meet one of our other teachers when class is over. She has some insight into things like that."

After the parents had picked up their children, Mrs. Cortez insisted that Alia meet Cathy Rutherford, the kindergarten teacher. She escorted Alia down the hall to Cathy's room just as she was tidying up.

Cathy looked to be about forty but didn't appear like the typical kindergarten teacher. She wore stylish makeup, earrings, bracelets, fashionable clothes, and a scarf around her neck. In other words, elegant. After a brief introduction, Mrs. Cortez explained that Alia felt unworthy of God's love due to some past experiences.

That's not how I put it, Alia thought to herself. *I was referring to the people, not God. Or Allah. Or whatever he is. Or IF he is.*

After the brief introduction, Mrs. Cortez left the room.

"So, what's going on?" Cathy asked.

"Oh, it's okay. It's overblown. Not much to talk about."

"It's just the two of us; and Dora – Mrs. Cortez – is good at reading people. So, what's up?" she asked again, smiling.

Why would I pour out my soul to a stranger, especially one who looks like she's all put together? Alia wondered.

At her hesitation, Cathy tried a different approach. "Maybe if I tell you a little about myself, it'll help. Do you want to sit down?" Cathy pointed to a chair made for a five-year-old. Alia shook her head no.

"When I was in my twenties, I spent ten months in jail for drugs. My husband, Bobby, spent two years in jail for that before we got married."

Alia looked at her in disbelief. Cathy was beautiful, stylish, and was a children's Sunday school teacher. *What could she have done that put her in jail?* "I look at you and I could never believe you've been in jail," Alia stated.

"I was a real party girl," Cathy continued, taking a seat on the edge of a table. "I smoked weed, did ecstasy and coke. I got it for my friends, too. That's the part that got me the jail time. By getting it for my friends, I was a dealer. Bobby was part of that party crowd, but we weren't dating at the time. Eventually, the cops busted him, and not long after that, they got me, too. My parents were Christians, and I went to church but I didn't really believe anything. Jail was a rude awakening. I'm a convicted felon, a reject of society, and a failure to my family. Who could love me?"

Yes, thought Alia, *that part I can relate to. Who could love me?* She sat down next to Cathy and looked at the floor rather than at Cathy. "I did some pretty nasty things. Not drugs, but other stuff. A family that goes to this church lets me stay with them and gave me a chance to start over. Then I met this guy and I started liking him; and when I thought things started to get serious, I told him about my past. He just got up and said he had to go home. He said he had to think about it. Now I just wonder if I'll ever be good enough; like if I'm just totally messed up for life."

Cathy turned towards Alia. "The answer is no, you're not messed up for life. God values you and when you understand that, it won't matter what people think. Some people may not come around, but you'll also find people who'll see you through God's eyes."

That's a nice message, but it sounds too religious to be useful, Alia thought. "What does that even mean?"

"It was someone at drug counseling who finally showed me the way. Have you heard about Rahab?"

"Like drug rehab?"

"No, not 'rehab', 'Rahab'; a woman in the Bible."

"Then, no."

Cathy retrieved her Bible from her oversized "mom" purse and flipped through the pages to a passage that must have been well known to her because she found it quickly. Alia thought she was going to start reading, but she just showed Alia where the name Rahab showed up. The header on the page said "Joshua."

"Rahab was a prostitute...," Cathy began.

Alia felt the hairs on the back of her neck stand up. *Did someone tell her about me?*

Cathy continued, "...and she was the only one in the city who believed in God. She helped two spies escape from the city and as a reward for her help, the Israelites spared her and her family's lives when they later attacked the city. That was way back in Jewish history. Then we jump forward to Jesus."

She turned to another passage in the Bible. Alia noticed that the header said "Matthew."

"Chapter 1 of Matthew gives us the lineage of Jesus. This passage starts with Abraham and ends with Jesus and tells us all the fathers in the lineage. It also provides a few notable mothers." This time she did read from the passage.

"It says, 'Salmon the father of Boaz, whose mother was Rahab….' That's the same Rahab from the book of Joshua. That means a prostitute is in the lineage of Jesus. That's when I realized that if Rahab could be worthy of God's favor, I could be, too. God loves people who are at the bottom of society.

"I found a husband. He was just as messed up as me, but that's another story. Even Rahab the prostitute found a husband. I'm not saying you'll find a husband, but the point is, no matter what you've done, if you have faith in God, He'll put people in your life who'll love you. It also helps if you stop doing the stuff that was messing you up."

When Alia finally left the kindergarten room, she found Emi waiting for her in the hallway. Emi had been sent to find out what was taking Alia so long.

"I hope you know we love you," Emi told Alia as she linked her arm with Alia's.

"You heard all that?"

"Only the last part. Mrs. Cathy was my Sunday school teacher when I was in kindergarten. She's nice."

"Did you hear her pray for me? That was kind of weird. It sounded like some kind of weird magic thing."

129

"I pray for you every night and I know Ty and Sophie do, too, 'cause I've seen your name on a list on Sophie's nightstand."

"I guess it's a good kind of weird. Thank you. You guys have helped me so much."

"How did you end up talking to Mrs. Cathy?"

"I kinda sorta told Mrs. Cortez that I was wondering if I could ever be accepted with my ugly past, but I didn't tell her what it was."

"Was that somehow related to your date with Caleb last night?"

"Yeah, he seems to have a hang-up about dating a prostitute."

"Former prostitute. That's a big difference."

Alia thought about the Lauren Daigle song that had become her favorite.

"How about 'rescued' prostitute?"

"That's even better."

As they walked to the foyer to meet up with the rest of the family Alia noted two things from the meeting with Cathy. *One: A convicted drug dealer was now teaching Sunday school to children. Two: God doesn't mind having a repentant prostitute in the line of the Christian messiah, the man described in Islam as a prophet of Allah. If God accepted her, others could, too. Now if only Caleb could see that.*

At the recommendation of Sophie and Ty, Alia decided to give Caleb time to figure things out. She would refrain from bombarding him with messages and wait for him to come around in his own time. After lunch, she decided Bob Barker needed to go for a walk.

Chapter 13
Holiday Celebrations

Alia knew many of the Christmas carols sung at the Christmas Eve service at church due to their popularity within society as a whole. The fact that she had been listening to a radio station that had inserted Christmas carols into their regular playlist since Thanksgiving helped with that familiarity. Like many in attendance, Alia especially liked the lighting of the candles. The service ended with the singing of "Silent Night" and the dimming of the overhead lights. The pastor lit a single candle and used it to light other candles that had been given to attendees as they entered the auditorium. Those holding the other candles touched their candles to yet others, thereby spreading the light from candle to candle throughout the auditorium. By the end of the song, the room glowed brightly with the light of hundreds of candles.

"That was neat," Alia stated to the Jensen/Butler family on the way home. "Jesus told his students to let their light shine for everyone to see. The candles reminded me of that.

Jesus told them about doing good deeds in the name of God so others would see God's goodness and would praise Him."

"I thought it symbolized people spreading God's message from person to person until everyone knows. But I like your idea, too. How did you know that?" Sophie asked.

"I've been reading the Bible."

"Really? On your own?"

"Yeah. I found some Bibles in a bookcase upstairs; the same place I found the Harry Potter books. After I talked with Mrs. Cathy, I wanted to see what it said about Rahab. That part about shining the light was near the beginning of the Jesus part."

"Jesus part? You mean, the New Testament?"

"Yeah, New Testament."

"What's rahab?" John asked.

"Jesus' great, great, great – lots of greats – grandmother."

"Why does she matter?"

"Because she was a prostitute."

"No way!"

"Really. I checked it out."

* * *

The family went to Ty's parents' house right after the service for a light dinner and to exchange gifts. Alia appreciated her employee discount at Bullseye. That helped with the small gifts she bought for the family. She opened one of her gifts to find a bikini inside.

"You'll need a swimsuit for the trip," Sophie explained. "I didn't know if you preferred a two-piece or a one-piece, but since you liked borrowing Emi's bikini top when you mowed the lawn, I went with a two-piece."

"That's cute," Ty's mother Amanda stated as Alia held up the top.

"Thank you, Sophie. I've never worn a bikini, but then, I haven't had any swimsuit in years."

"Oh. I can send it back, but I don't think we can get a one-piece delivered in time for the trip and the stores aren't selling swimsuits now."

"No. I like it. I want to keep it. I just meant my family was very conservative about how we dressed. In middle school, my parents got me and my sister burkinis – long sleeve swimwear for Muslim girls – but people would give us weird looks. So I just avoided swim events. Except for one time I didn't tell my parents I went to a pool party and I borrowed a friend's swimsuit; a one-piece.

"But I'll proudly wear this on the trip."

"Do you wanna try it on now?" John asked. "You know, to make sure it fits."

"John!" Sophie exclaimed. "As if you're really concerned about how it fits."

"Sure, John," Alia said, standing up. "Do you wanna come help me?"

John quickly stood up, grinning from ear to ear.

Alia started laughing. "I'm just kidding!" The whole family joined in the laughter. Except for John. The family couldn't miss the disappointment on his face.

"I got John on camera," Amanda laughed. "Before and after; happy face and sad face."

"Oooh, can you send those to me, Ms. Amanda?" Sophie asked.

Amanda looked at Sophie and cleared her throat.

"Oops. *Mom,*" Sophie giggled. "Can you send the pics to me, *Mom*?"

"That's better. It's been nine months already. The photos are on their way to you."

After receiving the iron press she requested for Christmas, Emi announced that she would be using it to make custom T-shirts for her recently rebranded YouTube channel, JentlerHair. She explained that the name is spelled with a "J", not a "G".

"Why 'J'?" asked Anna.

"The name's a combination of Jensen and Butler. J-E-N from Jensen and T-L-E-R from Butler," Emi explained. "I have to give credit to Ty 'cause he's the real reason people watch my videos."

"I am?" Ty asked, surprised.

"Yeah. YouTube has lots of videos of girls showing off their hairstyling, but not that many with a White man doing a Black girl's hair. Most of the comments are about Ty."

"Should I be happy or should I be concerned?" Ty asked, amused.

"Happy. You're like a celebrity and I got a lot more hits on the channel after I posted the video of you doing Sophie's hair a few weeks ago. I think it's 'cause the video includes Sophie's college friends. There were a couple of comments about the Prairie View shirt one of the girls wore, so I'm sure the girls showed their friends."

"I like the name," John stated. "Is that what you're gonna start calling us: the Jentler family?"

"I hadn't thought of that. It's just a YouTube name for now."

"I like 'Jentler'," Alia agreed. "Maybe I'll use it for you guys, even if you don't."

Emi beamed at the approval of her creativity.

* * *

On Christmas morning after breakfast and the opening of Santa's gifts, the Jensen/Butler – Jentler? – family escorted Alia to Ty's parents' house, where she would hang out with Ty's family for Christmas. That meant mostly hanging out with Anna and Bob Barker while the Jensen/Butler family made their annual overnight visit to the kids' grandparents in Dallas. It also meant finally trying on that swimsuit and the dresses and other clothes she received for Christmas, with Anna and Alia modeling their clothing bounty for each other. And Anna promised Alia a movie marathon for entertainment.

Alia couldn't help herself from texting "Merry Christmas" to Caleb, hoping the greeting would bring him back around. It took a couple of hours to get the same message back in reply. Just "Merry Christmas." She had hoped for more.

* * *

Aunt Ruth's and Ayo's wedding took place in Nigeria two days after Christmas. Aunt Ruth arranged for it to be live-streamed so her American friends and relatives could watch remotely. With the seven-hour time difference, that put the afternoon wedding at 7:00 am in Texas.

Sophie got up early enough to connect her laptop to the living room TV, turning it into a huge monitor. Then she called for the others in the household to wake up.

"It's a holiday and I don't even get to sleep in," John whined. "Why does the wedding have to be so early?"

"After all the times Aunt Ruth helped you with your homework, you can sacrifice a little sleep for her," Sophie replied.

Ty left for work even earlier than usual. Normally, he would be on the road at the time the wedding ceremony was going on. This day, he would get there early and watch it on his phone from the lunchroom. Fortunately, Alia's shift at Bullseye didn't start for a few hours, so she could see the whole ceremony and reception before work.

The ceremony was held in a church in Lagos with many elements that would have been familiar at an American wedding. The wedding clothes were a combination of western and traditional Nigerian clothing. Ruth wore a white wedding gown with plenty of beads. It was accented by an emerald green *gele* headwrap and matching green *iborun* shoulder sash, and further accessorized with a salmon-colored bead necklace. Ayo wore a grey tuxedo with green *fila* hat to match Ruth's *gele* and *iborun*.

Unfortunately, Ty couldn't watch the reception live, which took place at a hotel ballroom. He vowed to watch a recording of it after work. The reception was lively. Ruth and bridesmaids danced into the ballroom and Ruth twerked in front of Ayo.

"Your aunt's got some moves," Alia observed. "Sophie, you have to do that for Ty."

"How do you know I don't already?"

"Not while I'm around."

"Maybe it's a private thing."

"I think you should twerk for Ty when he comes home." Alia looked at John and Emi for their take.

"Yeah, that would be hilarious!" Emi exclaimed.

"Do you even know how to twerk?" John asked.

Sophie gave John a scolding look. Arms crossed, head tilted down and eyes looking up. If she had been wearing glasses, she would have been looking over them. Suddenly she flung her arms out and leaned forward, shaking her butt in a motion that ended with twerking. The other three screamed in amazement.

When the twerking ended, Alia looked up from her phone and said, "Got it."

"Were you recording me?!"

"Yes. I'm gonna show Dr. Ruth when she gets back. She needs to know how she inspired you." She smiled as an idea hit her. "You have to do that tonight when Ty comes home."

"Oooo. I'm gonna record his reaction," John stated.

Finally, the moment the kids were waiting for arrived. Unknown to Ruth and Ayo, the kids had recorded themselves performing two wedding songs, with John on piano and Sophie on violin. Emi sang the lead on "I Love the Way You Hold Me," by Jamie Grace, with John and Alia singing backup. They switched roles with P-Square's "No One Like You," with John singing the lead while playing the piano and Emi and Alia singing backup. They had all agreed that Ty should refrain from singing and concentrate on his guitar. Although he said he could sing and play at the same time, they insisted he stick to the guitar. Alia helped with percussion in the form of shaking a bottle of dried rice or clacking blocks of wood together at the right times. Sophie sent the videos to their grandmother who passed them on to the wedding coordinator. After the grand twerking entrance, their brief concert was displayed on a projector screen at the reception.

Ruth let out a squeal of surprised joy at the performance. Afterward, she ran to the live-stream camera.

"Sophie, Emi, John. I am very surprised. Thank you so much. I wish you could be here in person, but I am happy you could participate like this. Oh, and Ty and Alia, thank you, too."

* * *

When Ty walked in the door that evening, the other four members of the household were standing just inside the door with odd looks on their faces, as if they were waiting for something. Ty looked around puzzled.

Sophie stepped up. "Hi, Tiger." She said flirtatiously.

"Hi, Babe, why's everyone standing there looking at me?"

Suddenly music started coming from a speaker wirelessly linked to Alia's phone and Sophie began moving her arms and legs to the music. Suddenly, she turned her back to Ty, bent her knees, and thrust her bottom out. Then the twerking began.

Ty's eyes got big as he stared dumbfounded at his wife's moves. After a few lines of the music, she turned around and faced Ty, biting her lower lip and looking up at Ty through her eyelashes.

Without saying a word, he rushed forward, picked her up, and carried her to the bedroom.

"Hey!" Sophie shouted. "You need to shower first! You stink."

"We may be a while," he called out over his shoulder. They heard the bedroom door close.

"Is that how you thought he'd react?" Alia asked John and Emi.

"That's even better than I expected," John stated, laughing. "And I got it all on video."

"This is embarrassing," Emi said. "Well, I guess they *are* still newlyweds. Maybe we should give them some privacy and go out to dinner tonight. We can bring them back something."

"Hey, Sophie!" Alia shouted as she and the others left the house. "Make sure Ty watches Ruth and Ayo's reception!"

Chapter 14
The winter trip

Two days after the wedding the *Jentler* family left for their vacation to South Padre Island at the southern tip of Texas. Temperatures there were still in the upper seventies during the day, suitable for beach activities. They hitched the travel trailer to the Escalade, loaded it with all their gear, and, after having lunch and donning matching Jentler Hair T-shirts, hit the road. The shirts were Emi's creation using her new iron press. The shirts included the Jentler Hair logo, a line drawing of the top of a head from the eyes up with tight coils extending outward.

They planned to stop overnight in Corpus Christi and visit the Texas Aquarium the next morning, before going on to South Padre in the afternoon. A day on the beach, a New Year's Eve party at the Southern Tip Saloon and Grill, more beach, and return on January 2nd, the day before Alia's birthday.

"Why does John get to take a friend on the trip and I don't?" Emi asked on the way to Corpus Christi, from her seat on the middle row, behind Ty.

"You didn't ask," Ty responded.

"Emi doesn't have any friends," John teased from the back row.

"Hey, I know for a fact, Emi has friends," Lizzie interjected, elbowing John. "I'm one of them, and I met two at the karaoke party at your house last spring."

"And I'm another friend," Alia commented, patting Emi's leg. "See, Emi, you do have friends on the trip."

"Well, not my age. I could've invited Madison or Annie if I knew I could."

"Madison's too obsessed with sex, flirting with high school guys," John stated.

"She's not obsessed with sex. She just tells me what her older sister does."

"You mean her slutty sister," John retorted.

Sophie agreed with that point but kept her mouth shut. Emi had told her things about Madison's sister that hadn't been appropriate for Emi's age at the time.

"So, not slutty like me, huh?" Alia pointed out with faux offense.

"Uh... I mean... uh... not like you. You were forced into... uh...." John's voice trailed off.

"I guess that means I don't meet your standards? I'm not your type?"

"No. That's not what I mean."

"So, she *is* your type?" Lizzie asked John, who looked like he had just eaten something disgusting.

"I'm just teasing you," Alia explained. "I know what you mean. I didn't think at the time that I was being forced into the sex trade. The pressure was psychological. At least at first. It's like they brainwashed me into thinking I wanted to do it for the good of the group."

"Sounds like a cult," Lizzie said.

"Yeah, in a way, it is. They kept pushing ideas like, 'All the girls in the house are doing it;' and, 'we'll love you more if you help out;' and, 'you're not a virgin, so it's not like you're losing anything.' It's subtle so you don't know it's happening, but it built up. At first, I knew what they wanted me to do was wrong, and I didn't want to go along with it. But then I looked around and saw that the other girls were doing it. So it seemed like I was the only one thinking like that. Like, maybe I'm the wrong one, not them. It messes with your head."

Alia stared out the window, not at anything visible, but at the images in her mind.

She ran into the bathroom of the motel room and leaned over the toilet just in time for the contents of her stomach to erupt into the bowl. When there was nothing left to give, she curled up on the floor bathroom, sobbing. It was only the first night of her new occupation, and she'd only serviced two customers.

Bulldog came into the room and called out, "Alia, how's my girl?" He followed the sound of her sobs.

"I can't do this," Alia said between sobs. "I just can't."

Bulldog sat down on the edge of the bathtub and rubbed her back. "Yes, you can."

When she found her voice again, she reiterated, "No, I can't."

"I know it's hard at first, but you can." He slid off the tub and down onto the floor next to her. He put his arm under her and lifted her into a sitting position.

"One summer, I worked for a company that cleaned septic tanks. The truck didn't have A/C. The temperature was in the upper nineties and I would sweat buckets. The job was literally cleaning up other people's crap. It stank. I stank. When I got home in the evening, I could barely make it to the shower. I'd fall asleep on the sofa before dinner. It sucked. But each day, I got a little more used to it and it got a little easier. I needed the money. You know, food, rent, car payments, all that."

"I would rather do that," she sniffled.

Bulldog put his arm around her shoulders. "I'm just saying, you can get used to a job you don't like. It pays for your food, rent, clothes, and stuff. And you get air conditioning." He smiled at his attempted levity.

But the joke was lost on Alia. Her face screwed up for more sobs, but no sound came out this time. Eventually, she muttered, "I can't."

"Yes, you can. Only three more tonight. We're easing you into a full load." He pulled her up to a standing position, wrapped his arms around her, and kissed her lips. "My brave girl is strong. You can do this. Now let's get ready for the next customer."

She learned later that if Bulldog couldn't help the girls overcome their initial reluctance through encouragement, Blade and Shorty would help them overcome it with force. And when that force resulted in a girl missing a day of work, she would have to make up her quota of customers over the next few days.

Alia continued, "There's a point where it just seems easier to go along with what they want. Then it becomes routine. Until one day, you wake up and wonder who you really are, doing things you never considered doing before. At least, I woke up. Maybe some of the girls never do."

"Yeah, it does sound like a cult," Sophie agreed. "Alia, does it bother you to talk about that stuff? I mean, you were sort of making a joke about it with the 'slut' comment."

"I'll talk to you guys about it, but not to anyone I don't know well. I shouldn't have told Caleb yet. So let's just keep it within this family."

"Let's try to keep the discussions upbeat for now," Sophie stated. "We're on vacation to have fun."

Lizzie looked around at everyone in the vehicle before asking Alia, "Am I family?"

"Since you already know about me and you're with us all the time, you're included."

Lizzie smiled broadly and exclaimed, "Thank you, sis." She nudged John. "I'm family."

"Just don't call me brother," John replied. "That'd be creepy."

"How about 'Batman'?"

"I'll take that one."

* * *

After a fuel and restroom break, Lizzie made John sit in the middle row with Emi and asked Alia to join her in the back seat.

Thinking about family inclusion, Lizzie asked, "Do you like living with John's family?"

"Yes. They're fun, and there's no one yelling at them about being disappointed, or bringing shame to the family, or not putting out for the group."

"My parents don't yell. Well, not much. Mostly only if they think I'm not putting my best effort into schoolwork."

"Did they ever yell at you about who you date?"

"No. I only went out with two other guys before John. I only had one date with one of them and, like, three dates with the other one. So I don't count that as dating. And my dad likes John."

"That first time I took you out, your dad was cleaning his shotgun at the kitchen table," John interjected.

"You shouldn't be eavesdropping," Lizzie pointed out.

"I can't help it. You're only two feet away."

"That wasn't even my dad's gun. He borrowed it just to scare you."

"What!?"

Alia smiled at the image of Dr. Abboud trying to intimidate John with a shotgun. "Is this normal?"

"What? Trying to scare a daughter's boyfriend with a gun?"

"That's kind of like a joke. I get it. I mean, is it normal for you to get along with your parents."

"It's normal in *my* family," Lizzie said. "I know not everyone has a good home life. My friend's parents are getting a divorce and she said they fought a lot. But most have decent parents."

"John, did you get along with your parents?" Alia asked.

"Yeah. Except when it came to homework. Then Mom would yell a lot. Well, not really yelling, more like talking faster at a higher pitch. Mostly at me and Sophie, not Emi. Though, Dad yelled when I broke one of his golf clubs and when I spilled a drink in his car.

"But nowadays, it's Aunt Ruth who tells me she's disappointed if she thinks I'm not studying enough for calculus."

Bringing the discussion back around to her original question, Lizzie asked, "Are you gonna stay with John's family a while?"

"I don't know how long they'll let me. I mean, Sophie filled out my driver's license form with their address and they helped me register for school using their address. So I think they'll let me stay awhile."

"Hey Sophie," John called. "How long can Alia stay with us?"

Sophie looked at Ty before answering. He just gave a little shrug. "We haven't talked about how long that'll be. Alia, do you want to get through high school, and then we can reassess the situation?"

Ty added his thoughts. "Alia, we don't want to put any pressure on you or make you feel like we're controlling you.

When you and I were planning to get you back into high school, I didn't ask if you wanted to go back. I just sort of assumed you did and you didn't object. So I'll ask now: Do you want to finish high school?"

"Yes, I do. You weren't pushy. And I don't feel like you're trying to control me."

"The first few months I was helping this family, I had to learn how to advise without sounding pushy."

Emi jumped in. "Yeah, 'cause Sophie kept getting pissed off, thinking Ty was trying to take over."

"I wasn't pissed off," Sophie defended.

"Yes, you were," John and Emi responded simultaneously.

"In case you haven't figured it out," Ty said, "Sophie's the real boss in the family. I'm just here to be a blessing."

"Y'all are ganging up on me! I did have to learn to get over myself and realize Ty knew a lot more about life than I did. After a while, I realized I needed to defer to his better judgment. He's able to lead without acting bossy."

"Did anyone record that?" Ty asked. "But seriously, Alia, you can stay as long as you need. I don't want to be controlling, but if I think you're about to do something stupid that'll hurt someone in the family, I *will* put my foot down. I can't think of any examples, but if something like that came up, I'd try to talk you out of it and redirect your activity to something else. If that still didn't deter you, I might have to do something drastic."

"Ty, if that's supposed to sound intimidating, you don't do it very well," Alia stated. "So, if I brought over a bunch of girls and we started turning tricks out of your house, you'd stop it, right? Is that what you mean?"

"That's an extreme example, but that's the point I was trying to make."

"I get it and I appreciate you helping me with getting a driver's license and registering for school and everything."

"What is 'turning tricks'?" Emi whispered to Alia.

"What I did before John found me," Alia whispered back. "Getting paid to have sex."

* * *

After spending the morning and early afternoon at the Texas Aquarium in Corpus Christi, the group packed up and headed out to South Padre Island. On the way, Alia received a text message from an unknown number.

> Unknown:
> Hi. This is Andy. I know what
> you were involved in before
> you moved to our
> neighborhood. }${ Can we
> meet up?

Alia showed the message to Emi, who sat beside her on the drive.

"That's kinda creepy," Emi stated. "How would he know what you were involved in? And what do the brackets and dollar sign mean?"

Alia read the message out loud for all the vacationers to hear before she replied.

> Alia:
> Why? For sex? Screw
> yourself!

Can I call you to talk about
it?

> NO! Leave me alone!

"I can only think of one way he could know what I did. From Caleb." She texted Caleb.

Alia:
I can't believe you told Andy
about my past. I thought
you'd keep it private

> Caleb:
> I didn't tell Andy or anyone
> else

Liar!
Andy sent me a text that he
knows. How could he know
unless you told him? And
how did he get my number?

> I did give him your number,
> but I didn't tell him anything
> about you. I swear

Then why give him my
number?

He said he wanted to talk to
you about your past work. I
assume it's about mowing or
power washing

Tbh, I didn't pay too much
attention to the details
because he tends to ramble

I still don't know how he
could know about me unless
you told him. It's hard for me
to trust you now

"I guess it's really over between me and Caleb. I hoped he would get over my past and we could go out again. Now I feel betrayed and I don't even want to see him anymore."

"Forget about Caleb and Andy," Sophie stated. "We're on vacation. This trip is supposed to be happy and fun and Ty got us all reservations for a New Year's Eve party near the beach."

"Will we get to drink champagne at midnight?" John asked.

"Ty and I will, but you *children* will have to settle for ginger ale or Sprite." Sophie laughed as she emphasized the word children.

"Don't tell anyone outside of our group," Ty said mysteriously, "but there's a bottle of champagne in the trailer.

You young'n's can have some when we get back from the party."

"Cool," John replied. "At the party, how will they know who can drink and who can't?"

"Colored wristbands," Ty answered.

"Young'n's?" Alia repeated. "Is that a redneck term?"

Chapter 15
New Year's Eve

The trailer could comfortably sleep four; five if two were small children who got along well. For the three nights at South Padre Island, Ty had found a campground that also had small cabins. He booked a cabin for himself and Sophie and an RV spot where the rest of the group would stay. He had called the campground to ensure they could get an RV spot as close to the cabin as possible.

Unfortunately, the campground near Corpus Christi didn't have cabins available. Ty set up a tent and air mattress next to the trailer for himself and Sophie. John and Emi would get their usual spots at the rear of the trailer: John on the converted dinette bed and Emi on the drop-down bunk above the dinette. Lizzie and Alia would share the queen bed at the front.

As Lizzie watched Ty inflate the airbed in the tent, she commented to Sophie, "Newlyweds in a tent, huh? Are you gonna be able to keep the noise down so as not to disturb the other campers?"

"I appreciate your concern, Lizzie," Sophie replied in mock seriousness. "We'll try to contain ourselves for the sake of the other visitors in the park."

Lizzie's giggles turned into full fledge laughter as the other trailer inhabitants joined in. Ty completed the tent and mattress setup and looked puzzled at the sight of the five laughing travelers.

"Did I miss something?"

"Just girl talk," Sophie laughed.

John threw his hands in the air and shouted, "Hey! I'm here, too!" That just brought more laughter from the girls.

After attending to personal hygiene matters, Ty and Sophie left the trailer, turning off the outside lights as they closed the door. Ty continued onward to the tent, holding a flashlight, but Sophie stopped next to the trailer door. She put her face next to the wall and started moaning. Ty looked up with concern.

Sophie's moan increased in volume before she added "Yes! Yes!" Ty realized she was reenacting the restaurant scene in the movie *When Harry Met Sally*. In the scene, Sally demonstrated to Harry that a woman could fake an orgasm well enough to fool her partner. They had laughed with Aunt Ruth about the scene on one of her visits before she moved to Texas.

As Sophie wound up for the scene's climax, Lizzie opened the door and called out, "You guys are so embarrassing!"

Just then they heard a female voice from across the park call out, "I'll have what she's having!" The Jensen/Butler family burst out laughing, knowing that phrase came next in the movie scene.

"I'm glad there's another fan in the park," Ty stated.

Laughter could be heard from several sites within the campground.

* * *

It seemed like every hotel and bar on the island had a New Year's Eve party. Yet even with so many venues, the party at the Southern Tip Saloon was still crowded. Partly because the Southern Tip was one of the few venues that allowed teens. The crowd added to the excitement.

Alia observed that there were quite a few couples, which brought back thoughts of Caleb. Sophie had Ty and John had Lizzie; only Emi was unattached like her. Emi pulled Alia onto the dance floor to join her for a few songs. Two young teenage boys had been watching them, trying to work up the courage to ask them to dance. The boys had the same goal as all the single party guests, which was to find someone to be with at the stroke of midnight for the shout of "Happy New Year!" and, for the bolder guests, to get a New Year's kiss.

After a couple of dances, the two boys revealed themselves to be cousins who were in South Padre on vacation with their extended family. Both were fifteen years old and very happy to have found dance partners. Alia, however, didn't share Emi's enthusiasm. She was angry with Caleb for getting her hopes up for a real relationship, then betraying her. The only guys who showed interest were children; merely fifteen-year-olds. *I've had sex with more men than are in this room!* she mentally screamed to everyone in the place. *Isn't there at least one guy in here who would want to be with me on New Year's Eve?* Granted, most of the men she'd been with in her former career were old, overweight, or socially awkward. They would likely have been too timid to approach her in such a setting, and she would likely have turned them down, but that didn't dampen her bitterness. The large clock above the band showed only twenty minutes until midnight.

Alia looked down at the red wristband that signaled that she was under the legal drinking age, still a child. She tucked it up under the sleeve of her sweater. With a quick "excuse me" to Emi and the cousins, she walked towards the tables. Seeing an "adult" drink unattended on a table, she grabbed it and kept walking, gulping down the beverage as she walked.

She surveyed the room for potential partners. She saw a man in a denim jacket and western boots at the bar, holding a beer and talking to a man and woman who appeared to be together. The "cowboy", as Alia started thinking of him, didn't appear to have a date. No lipstick-smeared glass near him and no wedding ring. The couple headed for the dance floor, leaving him by himself.

Alia walked up and stood right in front of him. She set her empty glass on the bar and asked, "Are you finished with that beer, Cowboy?"

"Almost," he replied, smiling at the sudden attention from an attractive woman. Alia placed a forefinger against his shirt, near the collar, and ran the finger down his chest seductively.

Then she grabbed the beer from his hand and guzzled the remainder. "Looks like you're finished now."

She looked directly at him and smiled, almost daring him to respond, but the surprise of her boldness momentarily left him speechless.

"Can I buy you another one?" Cowboy asked when he got his voice back.

Alia hooked her left hand in the elbow of his right arm and said, "Let's dance," pulling him to the dance floor. He offered no resistance.

Sophie and Ty saw the action from across the room and sent a group text to the Jensen/Butler party.

> Sophie:
> It looks like Alia just picked up a guy. Keep an eye on her.
>
> Dance floor, near hallway to kitchen.

The band switched to a slow song as midnight approached and Alia put her hands on Cowboy's shoulders and swayed gently to the music. After a minute, he pulled her closer, looked down into her face, and kissed her. She reciprocated by placing her arms around his neck to keep him in that kissing position.

I don't need Caleb. I can get my own kisses.

The song ended and the screen behind the band displayed a countdown for the new year. When it reached ten, the crowd shouted out the countdown along with the screen. Alia and Cowboy didn't seem to notice. The midnight kiss would just be part of the passion they were jointly engaged in.

The Jensen/Butler crew moved to converge on the embracing couple during the countdown. At the stroke of midnight, Ty stopped and pulled Sophie in for a kiss; John pulled Lizzie in for a kiss; and one of the cousins pulled Emi in for a kiss, startling her. Emi paused in surprise, then shouted "Happy New Year" along with everyone else. She kissed the other cousin on his cheek so he didn't feel left out, then quickly left them to catch up with Ty and Sophie.

"You scared her off," the cheek-kissed boy said to his cousin.

"Why do you care? She kissed you, too."

Once Emi joined the family, Ty told them, "I'll go get the car. You see about Alia." Then to Emi, he said, "You come with me. No more kissing strangers."

After Alia and Cowboy paused their kissing long enough to shout "Happy New Year" along with the crowd, Cowboy pulled Alia in close to resume their dance floor make-out session as the band resumed its music.

Lizzie and John arrived first at the embracing couple. Lizzie told John, "I'll distract the guy and you get Alia. Just follow my lead."

Lizzie put her hands together and wedged them in between Alia and Cowboy. When they were sufficiently separated, she squeezed in and put her arms around Cowboy's neck, and kissed him.

John pulled Alia away and looked at his girlfriend kissing a stranger in bewilderment. He pulled Alia close, leaned down, and kissed her, keeping his eyes open to watch Lizzie. *She said 'follow my lead',* he thought.

Sophie arrived on the scene and gaped in amazement at the sight of Lizzie kissing Alia's dance partner and John kissing Alia. She grabbed Lizzie and Alia by their arms and shouted, "Come on!" over the sound of the music as she pulled them toward the exit. John followed close behind. They left a bewildered Cowboy standing in the middle of the dance floor.

Outside the Southern Tip, the music was muffled and the sound of fireworks could be heard in the distance over the Gulf.

Lizzie shouted at John, "Why did you kiss Alia?"

"I did what you did."

"I did that to distract the guy so you could get Alia away, not so you could kiss her. It worked for Anne Hathaway in *Get Smart.*"

"Is that a movie?"

"Ugh!"

Alia put her arms around John in a hug. "Thank you. I got kisses from two guys tonight." She looked pleased with herself.

"John's *my* boyfriend!" Lizzie exclaimed, not in anger, but to make a point. More softly, she said, "You'll get your own one day, but in the meantime, John's mine."

"Girls, you don't have to fight over me."

Lizzie raised her hand as if to slap him but then wagged her finger in his face. "No more kissing other girls."

Ty brought the Escalade around to the front and they all piled in. Emi was already in her place in the middle row. Lizzie climbed into the third row, followed by John. Alia surprised everyone by climbing into the back with Lizzie and John, sandwiching John between the two girls. Alia put her arm in the crook of John's.

Lizzie leaned forward and looked across John at Alia. "What are you doing?"

"Don't worry, it's a short ride. Just let me pretend for a few minutes."

Lizzie reached for John's hand and interlaced her fingers with his. John looked from side to side to get a look at each girl, then leaned back and smiled. Emi just shook her head in wonder.

"What's going on back there?" Sophie asked as she buckled herself in.

"Hormones," Emi replied.

* * *

Back at the campground, the group stood outside the trailer and drank champagne from red plastic cups while watching the fireworks. The official fireworks display had already ended, but individual groups of revelers were shooting off their own from boats in the Gulf. After a few minutes, Ty and Sophie retired to their cabin while the rest of the group went inside the trailer.

"I'm sorry, Lizzie," Alia apologized. "I'm not trying to take John away from you, but the attention felt good."

"Why were you hanging all over that stranger?" Emi asked.

"I didn't want to be alone on New Year's Eve."

Looking puzzled, Emi responded, "You weren't alone, you were with us."

"I wanted to be kissed. I wanted to feel wanted." Alia paused. "You know, one of the big reasons men hire girls like me is because they're lonely and can't get dates on their own. I kind of know how they feel, after Caleb."

"Caleb's an idiot. There'll be another guy for you," Lizzie said. "But it's not John."

"I know. Although John is cute and he's a good kisser."

At that Lizzie crossed her arms and gave Alia a stern look.

"You two are so lucky. To make it up to you, I've got an idea." Alia walked to John at his position on the edge of his dinette-turned-bed and grabbed his arm.

"Stand up and follow me," she commanded, pulling him towards the front of the trailer, next to the big bed.

"You sleep with Lizzie tonight. You need to show her some love."

"I'm not gonna have sex in a room full of people, one of whom is my sister."

"I don't think he's ever had sex at all," Emi pointed out.

"And I'm not starting tonight."

"I never said anything about sex. You can just cuddle and fall asleep together."

"That's okay, Alia," Lizzie said. "I appreciate it, but I think we should just stick with our usual sleeping arrangement."

"Yeah," John agreed. "Otherwise, one day I'll be at Lizzie's house and the next thing you know, I'll wake up with no teeth."

"What does that mean?" Alia asked.

"My dad's a dentist," Lizzie explained. "It's something he told my other dates. 'If you mess with my daughter, I'll pull all your teeth out,'" she said, trying to mimic her dad's voice.

"He may have been kidding, but I'm not taking any chances," John said.

Chapter 16
Andy's discovery

During the ride home, Alia received a new text from another unknown number.

> Unknown:
> Hi Alia. This is Shelby, Andy's cousin. We met at dinner a few weeks ago. Andy would like to meet you for coffee, but it seems that he got stupid and didn't know how to ask you.

> Alia:
> His message sounded rude. Did he ask you to contact me?

> It was my idea for him to reach out to you in the first place. Andy can be a pain in the butt sometimes but he means no harm. Despite all

of Andy's stupid stunts, he
can be a good friend. And it
never hurts to have another
friend.

If I was in town, I'd join you,
too. But I'm still in Arkansas.

Alia read the messages out loud to the other occupants of the vehicle.

Sophie summarized, "Andy told Shelby he knows something about Alia, and Shelby told him to set up a date? I assume Shelby's not interested in helping Andy get sex. This whole thing is kind of mysterious."

Shortly after the messages from Shelby, Alia's phone vibrated to signal another message.

Andy:
I just realized my texts could
be taken the wrong way.
Shelby pointed out how bad
it sounded.

Just coffee.

Will you have coffee with me
in the middle of the day at a
public coffee shop?

Alia read the texts out loud again. "What do you think I should do?"

"I want to see where this story is going," Sophie said.

Alia turned to look behind her at Lizzie to get her opinion.

"Let me see your phone," Lizzie requested. Alia handed it over so Lizzie could read the messages for herself. Lizzie began typing.

> Alia:
> Sure. Starbucks near Best
> Buy. Tomorrow @10am.

"Hey!" Alia protested. "What are you doing?"

"Setting up the meeting," Lizzie explained, handing the phone back to Alia. "We all want to know what's going on. You'll meet Andy at ten tomorrow and Sophie and I can 'coincidentally' be having coffee at the same shop at the same time."

"How do you know I'm available at ten tomorrow?"

"Are you?"

"Yes."

"Can I come, too?" Emi asked no one in particular.

"Come on," Alia whined. "Is this like a Jentler family event?"

"Jentler family?" Lizzie asked.

"Jensen. Butler. Jentler. Like Emi's shirts."

"Oh, that's what that meant. I thought Emi was just advertising her video channel."

"Does that mean John and I can come, too?" Ty asked.

"Sure. Why don't we invite your parents and Bob Barker, too?" Alia replied.

"I don't think they allow dogs," John stated.

Lizzie and Alia rolled their eyes.

* * *

Alia and the Jensen girls arrived at Starbucks early and met Lizzie. Alia waited outside near the door for Andy as the others placed their orders and staked out a table inside. They had never met Andy, so he wouldn't likely know they were there to keep an eye on Alia.

Andy arrived promptly at ten. He started to move in for a hug and Alia turned to the door and said, "Let's go inside."

After placing their orders, a time in which Alia couldn't tell if Andy was flirting with the barista or just being overly friendly with her, they found an empty table and sat down. Unfortunately for the spies, the table wasn't near enough to the others for eavesdropping.

"What did Caleb tell you about me?" Alia asked bluntly.

"Nothing. I knew there was something wrong between you two when he mentioned he needed a date for a New Year's Eve party, but when I asked why he didn't take you, he just said y'all didn't work out."

"Not that I was going out of town, but that we 'didn't work out'?"

"That's what he said."

"What else did he say about me?"

"Nothing. Then we started talking about football."

Alia folded her arms and leaned back in her chair. Andy's answer corroborated what Caleb had said about not telling Andy anything. *How else would Andy know my past? Did I jump to conclusions? Did Andy truly know anything about my past?*

"Okay. Your text said you knew about my past. What do you know?"

Before answering, Andy took off his jacket and rolled up his left sleeve.

"What do you think?" he asked.

"About what?"

"My tattoo," he said, pointing to the lightning bolt tattoo on his bicep. "I'd been telling people I wanted to get a tattoo."

"I remember you said that a few weeks ago."

"So, for Christmas, my brother gave me an IOU for a tattoo. Then he took me to a tattoo shop. So, what do you think?" he repeated.

"Nice," Alia responded, still wondering when he would answer her question.

"Lightning bolt. You know, high energy, like me."

Does high energy mean going off on tangents?

The barista called out their names to let them know their coffees were ready. As Andy left to get the drinks, Alia turned to the spies and gave a small nod of acknowledgment.

When Andy returned, Alia asked, "What does your tattoo have to do with me?"

"So, at the tattoo place, they have a lot of pictures and posters on the walls. Most were examples of tattoos they had done, but one poster showed tattoos that required the owner's approval. One of the examples was the same tattoo you have on the back of your neck. I tried to put that in the text. The dollar sign with butterfly wings."

"Ooohhh. The bracket-dollar-bracket. I wondered what that meant."

"I thought it was obvious. Anyway, I asked what was so special about those tattoos that required approval. The guy said they were commonly used for, um, for…you know, girls who…" His voice trailed off.

"Prostitutes."

"Yeah. They're sort of a brand for the pimp."

"So, why point it out to me?"

"You've been mowing lawns in Caleb's neighborhood, so I assume you're no longer a… um…."

"Prostitute."

"Right. And something happened between you and Caleb. I mean, one day he was excited to be going out with you, and the next day, when I asked how the date went, he said you'd been involved in some heavy stuff."

"So he did talk about me."

"That's it, 'heavy stuff.' He wouldn't elaborate. A few days later he's said he needs a date for New Year's Eve."

"Right," Alia uttered, still skeptical.

"I told Shelby about the tattoo and how Caleb was acting. She said maybe you could use a friend. Since she wasn't in town, I'm her proxy. I mean, I'm not just doing it for Shelby; I could use another friend, too. You can never have too many friends."

"Okayyyy," Alia drew out the word.

Andy picked up his phone and scrolled through his text messages, looking for something specific. He landed on the texts from his first contact with Alia.

"I'm not trying to have sex with you and screwing myself doesn't work. I always wondered if intersex people could do that. I mean, could they fit one part into their other part and get themselves pregnant?"

While looking down into her coffee, Alia gave a small snicker, partly at his joke and partly at another example of him going off subject.

She looked up and said, "I'm sorry for thinking the worst and saying that, but you have to admit that your message was … uh… poorly worded."

"I know I can come across as rude sometimes. I'm always saying outrageous stuff for a laugh and Shelby reminds me how stupid I sound. That's just me. In high school, I would drink a lot and do stupid things for attention. For laughs. Most of the time it worked. I still do stupid things for laughs, but I cut down on the drinking."

"Wait. You went to college and cut down on drinking? Isn't that what college students do? Have parties and get drunk?"

"Yeah. That's what most do, but it was the opposite for me. That's a story for another time."

"I'd like to hear it sometime."

"Does that mean there will be another time?"

Alia smiled. "For Shelby's sake."

"Changing the subject," Andy said, "how were your holidays?"

* * *

On the car ride home, Alia summarized the entire conversation for Sophie, Lizzie, and Emi.

"So, Andy's not the bad guy you thought he was?" Lizzie asked.

"No. And maybe Caleb's not as bad as I thought, either. I mean, he still ghosted me, but he didn't tell Andy about me like I thought."

"I hope you're not still thinking you'll get back together with him," Sophie stated with a questioning tone.

"No. I'm over him. I'm moving on." She thought about Rahab and wondered if she was rejected before finding a husband.

"What were y'all laughing about?" Emi asked.

"I was telling him about our trip. Sophie's moaning episode, how I picked up a guy for New Year's Eve, and how Lizzie and John 'rescued' me. He thought that was hysterical. He said y'all – we – must be a really fun group. Then he told me about his family's tradition of pranking family members by passing around the same pair of pants to a different person each Christmas. This year it was inside a fishing tackle box that his dad gave his uncle. One time, someone baked it into a cake. That, and they all wear ugly Christmas sweaters."

"It sounds like his family is pretty fun, too. Remember, we're having your birthday dinner at Ty's parents' house tonight. Why don't you invite Andy?" Sophie said.

"Let me see your phone," Lizzie stated and held out her hand.

"I can do it this time," Alia replied as she began texting Andy.

"I hope he comes," Emi expressed. "I wanna hear about the Christmas pants."

* * *

The stairway wall got a new photo: a group shot of the family at a beach in South Padre Island.

Chapter 17
Back to school

The winter break ended for the local schools and John and Emi would be returning to school, while Alia was starting fresh. Sophie had another two weeks before her classes resumed. Emi would be taking the bus to middle school, while John got to drive himself. Alia's school, the Bauman Center, had programs specially designed to help students catch up on the credits needed to graduate. It catered to those who missed considerable amounts of school for various reasons. One could graduate from the Bauman Center or could transfer to one of the traditional high schools in the district once the credits were sufficiently caught up. The challenge facing the Jensen/Butler family was that the school was about a 25-minute drive from home and had no bus service. It was also in the opposite direction from Ty's job and Sophie's college.

For the first two weeks, Sophie could take Alia to school in the mornings and could pick her up in the afternoons. After that, Sophie was limited to mornings only. They had two weeks to figure out how Alia would get home after Sophie returned to college.

This became one of the discussion topics at Alia's birthday dinner at the Butler's house. The thought of going back to high school gave Alia a new sense of excitement and a little bit of anxiety.

"I can pick her up each day until A&M starts back up," Andy offered. "Then we could hang out after school."

"That works for me," Alia replied, looking to Sophie for affirmation.

"Didn't you just tell us you were a little concerned about getting back into the habit of schoolwork and everything?" Sophie asked.

"Yeah."

"Would Andy be a distraction if you have homework in the afternoons? Especially when you're first settling in?"

"Well, maybe."

"It's your call, Alia," Ty interjected. Sophie shot him a dirty look.

"Thanks, Andy, but maybe Sophie should pick me up so I can concentrate on school."

"What about Fridays?" Andy asked. "There are two Fridays until I have to go back."

Alia looked at Sophie, who nodded.

"Sure, you can pick me up on Fridays and we can hang out."

"Superb! Friday, it is."

"Hey, Andy," Emi called out. "Tell us about the pants that your family re-gifts every Christmas."

"Did Alia tell you about that? It's hilarious. Well, one year, one of my uncles was wearing these really ugly pants. They had these, like, vertical red and blue stripes. He called them hippy pants, but they looked more like clown pants to me. He wore them as a joke to go with his ugly Christmas sweater. My dad said they looked great and he wished he had a pair. He was being sarcastic. Well, the next year, his Christmas present from my uncle was the ugly pants. The year after that, my dad gave them back, but he put them inside a golf bag. So, my uncle still got a decent gift, but that started a whole tradition of passing the pants around between my uncles, my grandfather, and my dad. Usually hiding them in something else. It's been going on for, like, ten years and now they're threatening to include me."

* * *

Alia started school with the "Priceless" sweatshirt Emi had made for her birthday. It was a pink sweatshirt onto which Emi had used her iron press to iron on the word "Priceless" across the front in white cursive-style lettering. She paired it with a gray skirt and black leggings. Alia topped off the look with a pink ribbon in her hair. Looking at herself in the mirror before school, she looked forward to warmer weather when she could dispense with the leggings and just wear a skirt. She wouldn't have been able to get away with bare legs back in St. Louis. Her strict parents wouldn't have let her out of the house like that.

Ty drove her to school that first day since he had been with her to register for classes a few weeks earlier. He wanted to check in with the registrar to make sure everything was in order. Sophie met her in the afternoon to pick her up.

"How'd your first day go?"

"I already got a ton of homework. I expected the first week to be easy. That's how it was at my old school, but this is like two semesters squeezed into one."

"You've got us to help. Did you make any friends?"

"I met a lot of people. At lunch, I met a girl who missed a lot of school because she had cancer and now she's trying to catch up; and a guy who just wants to graduate early and start working full time; and two guys who had moved around a lot and got behind in school. I think some of them just dropped out because they weren't good at school and later decide to go back, like Ty's case."

"Did you meet anyone who lives near us?"

"I don't know. We didn't talk about where we lived."

"Try to find out if anyone lives close to us and would be willing to give you a ride. I mean, I can do it through next week, but then we have to figure something out."

* * *

School and homework left Alia with a very busy schedule. She still wanted to work but had to limit it to the weekends until she got used to the school workload. Besides, the lack of transportation during the week would have made the trip to Bullseye more difficult.

Ty grilled her each night on her homework progress and upcoming homework due dates. She hadn't expected Ty to be the one most concerned about her academics, but John was the person most helpful with the actual homework. While he used to do his homework in his room, this semester he started joining Alia at the kitchen table for homework sessions.

"You don't have to babysit me," she said.

"I wanted to be nearby in case you needed help with your homework. You know, 'cause it's been a while since you've been in school."

"I think I can handle it."

"Fine. But since I'm already here, I'll just quietly do my own homework."

Alia shuffled through several papers before finally settling on one to concentrate on. She began writing in a notebook.

"Look at this homework question. What do you think the teacher means…?

"So you do need help?"

Alia glared at John for a few seconds before repeating, "So, what do you think the teacher means on that question?"

* * *

Andy picked her up on Friday. He took a different route than Sophie had been taking and his route went past the shopping center where Alia and Lizzie had previously seen the ugly truck for sale. It was still there, but the price changed. The owner had drawn a line through the $1,200 price on the sign and scribbled $1,000 underneath.

"It's still there," Alia stated.

"What's still there?"

"That truck is still there. Lizzie and I stopped to look at it a couple of months ago."

Andy pulled into the shopping center and doubled back to park beside the ugly truck.

"It's pretty obvious why no one wants it. It looks like it's been hit a few times."

"Well, it must be drivable. Last time, it was parked closer to the other end of the shopping center."

They got out and walked around the truck. Andy peered into the cab and began laughing. "Hand crank windows. That's rare. And look at the gear shift. That's a manual transmission."

"What does that mean?"

"When you increase speed, you have to manually shift from low speed to higher speed. You have to step on that pedal on the left and move the gear shift."

"I still don't get it."

"Most cars and trucks have an automatic transmission and they shift gears without you even knowing it, but race cars and Italian sports cars have manual transmissions. They say a human can shift gears better than the automatic, but maybe it only matters for racing."

"Do you know how to use it?"

"Yeah, but it's been a couple of years. The owner of the deer lease my dad uses has an old farm truck with a manual transmission and he let me drive it around the property. Most people don't know how to use it. That's probably another reason why no one wants it."

"It's still out of my price range."

* * *

They drove through the smoothie shop and purchased three smoothies. Alia wanted to buy one for Emi and even tried to pay for it herself, but Andy insisted on paying. They continued their conversation at the Jensen home. After catching Andy up on school activities and listening to him have an anecdote for seemingly every topic she brought up, Alia pointed out, "You don't have to have a comeback for everything I say. Sometimes you can just listen."

"Sorry, I tend to run on and on."

"It's okay. Sometimes, I just want to listen, sometimes I want to be listened to, and sometimes it's okay to be quiet."

"I don't know if I can be quiet."

"So I've seen. Then tell me how you gave up alcohol for college."

"I never said I gave it up. I just don't get drunk anymore. It started last summer before college started."

"Feel free to ramble on. I'm in listening mode."

"I was that guy at the parties who always got drunk and did stupid things. People expected it. They would dare me to do something and I would do it."

"Like what?"

"One time I jumped off the roof into the pool. With my clothes on."

"That seems kind of cliché."

"Another time, I swallowed a live goldfish from this guy's fish tank. I've had sushi, so I didn't think it could be any worse than that."

"Eww. That's animal cruelty."

"Is it any worse than fishing?"

"What happened to make you drink less and give up the stupid stunts?"

"Oh, I still do stupid stunts. Well, maybe not quite as stupid, but still stupid. There was this graduation party in the summer. No parents home; I drank a lot, as usual; and there was this girl there that I didn't know, but she was pretty drunk, too.

"My friends dared us to make out with each other. They shoved us into a closet and closed the door.

"Anyway, the next day, my friends said that we were doing more than just making out, if you know what I mean."

"Meaning, you went all the way."

"That's what they said. I have no memory of it at all, which was scary. I didn't even know the girl, and I don't carry a condom in my wallet like some guys."

Alia nodded, remembering Caleb showing her the condom packet from his wallet.

"In my sober state, my mind went all serious. Did we really have sex? Did she get pregnant? Would there be a little Andrew or Andrea in nine months?"

"So, what did you do?"

"I asked around and eventually found out who the girl was. I found out she was fine and not pregnant. Her friends made her get the morning-after pill. She had no memory of it either. She was actually pretty hot, so I'm really disappointed I can't remember anything. Anyway, that shook me up enough to never want to lose control so much that I affect other people like that."

"I'm sorry that happened. Did you try to go out with her?"

"I asked and she said no. Maybe she was embarrassed about what happened or she thinks she's out of my league."

"And I'm not out of your league? Because of my dark past?"

"Normally, I'd say you're out of my league, but you invited me to your birthday party, so maybe I moved up a step."

"Do you like basketball?" Alia asked abruptly.

"Sure, sometimes I join a pickup game at the gym."

"I mean, watching basketball."

"Yeah, that, too."

"Good, let's go to the Cy Grove basketball game tonight. John's playing."

"Is this a date?"

"If you want it to be."

181

"I'm in." *Yep, I've moved up a step.*

* * *

Another photo appeared on the stairway wall; the second one that did not include anyone with the last name of Jensen or Butler. The photo showed Alia at the entrance of the Bauman Center on her first day of school.

Chapter 18
The ride

On Monday Alia met two students who lived nearby and when she brought up the possibility of getting a ride home after school, both volunteered. Alia said maybe they could alternate so she didn't become a burden. Dina said she would need to run it by her mother first, so Alia chose Gil for the first ride. She texted Sophie that she had found rides home.

After school, Gil insisted they stop by a burger shop before going home. Alia thought he intended to go through the drive-thru and was surprised when he pulled up and parked. She followed him inside, though she wasn't hungry and just wanted to go home. Despite her protests, he ordered an extra drink and extra French fries for her. She spent the next thirty minutes listening to him talk about video games and how his cousin could supply weed if she needed any. His difficulty in picking up social cues was obvious.

Or is he just ignoring my stated desire to go home? Alia thought.

The next day he mentioned their "date" to others at school. *At least Dina would be providing the ride this time.*

Dina was better at conversation than Gil and kept it on a superficial level. She drove directly to the Jensen house with no stops along the way, even when there should have been. Alia noted, with gritted teeth and white knuckles on the door handle, that Dina drove through a red light and two stop signs. She might have sped through a school zone had the traffic not forced her to slow down.

After those first two days, Alia wasn't sure which was worse, the socially awkward Gil or the demon driver Dina. Maybe she would be more certain after Wednesday's ride. It was Gil's turn again. This time, instead of stopping for food, he drove to his house. He wanted to show Alia his gaming setup and thought they could hang out since they hadn't stopped for food. When Alia insisted she needed to go home to start on homework, Gil said the stop would be brief. He thought she would be impressed with his gaming system. Alia kept her phone in the ready position to make an emergency 9-1-1 call if necessary, but after she expressed faux admiration in his gaming equipment, Gil was sufficiently satisfied and took her home. The next day he mentioned to others that he and Alia hung out at his house.

"Today Gil moved from awkward to creepy," Alia told Emi after describing the experience.

Thursday, Dina announced that she wouldn't be able to drive that day because she'd been in a small accident the day before and her dad would work on the car over the weekend. Alia texted Sophie for a ride.

Friday, Andy once again met her at school. His slight awkwardness came from talking too much but wasn't on the creepy level of Gil's; he also drove better than Dina.

They once again drove past the ugly truck. It still had the 'for sale' sign. Andy noticed Alia staring at it again.

"Do you want to stop and look again?"

* * *

When Ty arrived home after work, he recognized Andy's car parked at the curb behind an ugly old small-body pickup. Once in the house, he looked around for the guests. He saw Andy and Alia excitedly talking with Sophie, John, and Emi. He glanced toward the hallway bathroom to see if the driver of the truck might be using it, but the door was open and the light was off.

"Who's truck is that outside?"

The four people who weren't Alia all pointed to her.

"I can drive myself to school now!" Alia exclaimed. Then she added, "Do you know how to drive a stick shift?"

"It's a stick shift?"

"Yes. I need to practice on it. Do you know how?"

"Yeah. Did someone give it to you?"

"I bought it. The sign said $1,000…" Alia started.

"But I talked 'em down to $800," Andy finished.

"So, you're part of this?"

Before Andy could answer, Alia stated, "I know it's ugly, but it runs. Andy drove it home and I drove Andy's car."

"Are you sure it's worth $800?"

"It runs," she repeated. "And I don't have to ride with creepy Gil and demon Dina. Can you help me practice?"

"What about Andy?"

"I've got something with the family most of the day tomorrow," Andy explained. "My cousin Shelby's back in town and the family wants to get together, and Sunday I'm heading back to College Station for school." He looked hopefully at Alia, "But I'm free tomorrow evening."

"Alright, I'll help you practice, Alia," Ty conceded. "I may be a bit rusty since it's been years since I drove a stick, but I'm sure it'll come back to me. We can practice on the ramps at the bus center garage. The garage will be empty on the weekend."

"Great!" She practically bounced when she said it.

Ty called the insurance company to add the ugly truck to the family's policy.

* * *

Saturday morning, Ty and Alia practiced driving. It was one thing to hear the concept of manually changing gears; it was quite another to feel the vibrations of the engine reverberating through the steering wheel or the shift lever and know when to make the change. Ty explained that she could watch the RPM gauge to see when the needle reached the level needed to shift gears, but the best method was to feel it. It took a while for Alia to get used to using her left foot on the clutch pedal. After several jerking motions that caused the engine to die, Alia got the hang of it. The next step was to practice starting and stopping on the inclines in the parking garage.

By the early afternoon, Alia felt comfortable enough to drive to Bullseye on her own for work.

* * *

Andy and Shelby met Alia in the Bullseye parking lot after her shift ended Saturday evening. Upon seeing Alia's truck, Shelby began laughing and had a hard time stopping. She punched Andy in the arm.

"How could you let her buy that?"

"It runs," Andy and Alia said simultaneously.

"But for how long?"

Alia insisted on driving both of them to dinner.

"There are three of us and there's no back seat," Shelby pointed out.

Alia opened the passenger door and showed her the interior. "The middle armrest folds up so someone can sit in the middle. Go ahead and get in." Shelby looked at Andy to see if he found anything wrong with the proposed seating.

"It even has three seat belts. Come on," Andy said, climbing in first and seating himself in the middle, with one foot on each side of the floor-mounted gear shift. Shelby, still unsure of the bench seat concept, hesitated before getting in and closing the door. Alia got in the driver's seat, closed her door, and started the engine.

As if Andy hadn't already explained the whole purchase process to Shelby, he launched into the story again.

"Last week, Alia wanted to stop and look at the truck, so we did a walk-around. And yesterday, we drove by again, and she kept staring at it, so I turned into the parking lot to check it out again. Alia complained that she still couldn't afford to pay $1,000, but I started calling the number on the sign anyway."

Alia reached over and put her hand over Andy's mouth, and said "Shh." Andy responded with a mumble.

"This is my story. Let me tell it," Alia insisted.

"If I knew it was that easy to shut him up, I would've used that method a long time ago," Shelby stated.

With her hand still over Andy's mouth, Alia asked, "Are you gonna let me talk now?"

He nodded. She removed her hand.

"The owner works in a sandwich shop in that shopping center. He's an old guy who'd been saving the truck for his grandson, but the grandson didn't want it."

"Probably 'cause it's so beat up," Shelby said.

"He didn't get much interest in the truck from potential buyers. He said one guy offered $500 for scrap, but since it still ran, the owner held out for a better offer.

"That's when Andy blurted out $800 without even asking me. And the guy agreed! So, Andy drove me to the bank to get the cash and we went back and bought the truck. But I didn't know how to drive a stick shift, so he drove the truck home and I drove his car."

"Wait. Andy let you drive his Camaro?"

"Yes."

"You wouldn't let me drive it," Shelby commented, looking at Andy.

"We didn't have much choice here. She couldn't drive the truck."

"I practiced driving this morning. So now I have my own ride. Shelby, check this out." She pointed to the clutch pedal. "You have to step on that pedal to change gears."

Alia reached for the shift lever, put it into reverse, and release the clutch. The truck lurched as her clutch and shift work were still not refined, but at least it moved backward as intended.

"You'd better watch your jewels when she shifts into third," Shelby said to Andy.

"Maybe I'm looking forward to a little physical contact," he replied.

Shelby elbowed him in his right side.

Alia elbowed him in his left side.

* * *

Alia smiled a little more at church on Sunday than usual. After helping with the toddlers, she stopped by Cathy's classroom to say hello. She had meant to do that last week, as well, but at that time Cathy was deep in conversation with a parent so Alia just waved and continued on without greeting.

Alia had become more comfortable with the church routine. Much of the terminology still sounded foreign, but at least she knew what to expect. After the first couple of weeks, she even began standing along with the congregation during the music and had learned the words. A few weeks after that, she found herself inadvertently mouthing the words of the songs. When she realized what she was doing, she stopped, but then the next week, it happened again.

"How's it going, Alia," Cathy greeted.

"You remembered my name," Alia said, impressed.

"Of course. It's hard to forget when I've been praying for you. Has the situation improved?"

"Well, I made a new friend. Actually, I already knew him and thought he was annoying. But now we're friends."

"That's great! What about that other guy you were upset with?"

"That's over, but in other news, I had a nice trip to South Padre for New Year's, I started school – two weeks now – and," she paused for effect, "I bought a truck!"

"Awesome! I'm really glad things are going well for you!"

Was it due to the prayers or just a lucky series of ordinary events?

"When we talked before Christmas, I got the impression you don't come from a church background."

Alia tensed up. She wondered if she was about to be exposed as an imposter, a Muslim atheist whom everyone here thought was a Christian. She never claimed to be a Christian, but merely responded to a call for help with the toddlers.

"On Sunday nights, I meet with a group of young people at Paolo's Pizza near the movie theater to talk about what it means to be a Christian. Most of them don't come from a

Christian background. Some aren't Christians but are just checking it out, and some are new Christians who still don't understand much of what they hear in church. So we talk about the basics, and everyone's free to be skeptical." She pulled out a piece of paper from a notebook and began scribbling, then handed the paper to Alia.

"That's my phone number. 7:00 pm tonight and every Sunday."

Alia couldn't recall if she'd told Cathy that she wasn't a Christian. "Do you know my background?"

"You said you used to do bad things and thought people couldn't love you because of it, but also that you're living with members of this church. That's about all I know. Maybe it's time to find out what your friends are putting their faith in. We'll be at Paolo's in the back corner."

* * *

After lunch, Alia excused herself and paid a visit to the hardware store. When she returned, she had several cans of house paint, brushes, rollers, and other paint supplies. She pulled up in the driveway next to Ty's truck and arranged her supplies on the driveway. She started applying masking tape around the windows, door handles, and trim of her truck. By the time John finally came outside to see her activity, she had nearly finished the taping.

"What are you doing?"

"Getting ready to paint the truck."

"You're gonna paint it with a brush? You're supposed to use spray paint on cars. Besides, that's house paint."

"So? It's exterior paint, so it shouldn't wash off in the rain. And I'll use rollers. Don't criticize. I'm still making my truck beautiful."

"If you have an extra roller, I can help."

"I bought two, just in case."

"What color did you get?"

"First, we'll paint it with white primer. Then we'll paint it pink."

"Pink? Seriously? No one paints a truck pink."

"Why not? I want pink. Now help me tape the dropcloth to the driveway around the truck to keep it from blowing away."

"I see you have some black paint, too," he said, holding up a spray can.

"The black spray paint is for the bumpers. The black brush paint is for some designs I plan to make."

"Got it. You hold that end of the dropcloth and I'll stretch it out."

By sunset, the previously green and black truck sported a fresh coat of white primer. Alia called the whole family outside to see the results of the first phase of the beautification plan.

"It's already looking a lot better than before," Emi proclaimed. "Too bad the new paint won't hide the dents."

Alia had forgotten about Cathy Rutherford's invitation.

* * *

Although eager to continue the paint job, Alia would have to wait until Tuesday. Ty insisted that she get the title transferred right away, so on Monday Alia spent the afternoon at the vehicle registration office at the county courthouse annex. Ty had looked online for the required documents, so she felt somewhat prepared. She wished Emi or John could have come with her, but John had basketball practice, and going home after school to get Emi would have caused an hour delay. By the time she had returned home with new license plates, there wasn't enough time to paint a full coat of pink before sunset. *Ty would probably have been on my case about schoolwork, anyway*, she thought. Getting the vehicle registered took higher priority than painting on the list of study-time exceptions.

"Ty, can I borrow a screwdriver to put on my new license plates?"

"Sure. Come with me to the garage."

As they walked out to the garage, Ty pointed out, "This morning after you left, I noticed some oil spots on the driveway where your truck had been parked. Did the guy you bought it from say anything about oil leaks?"

"Oh, yeah. He said he had to add a quart of oil every couple of months because of a leak. He said someday it'll need a new casket."

Ty almost laughed out loud at the thought of the truck dying and needing to be buried in a casket. He stifled the laugh into a small cough. "Do you mean gasket?"

"Yeah. It'll need a new gasket, but it runs fine for now."

"Let's find a pan to put under the engine to catch the oil drips when you park in the driveway. If you parked this at my parents' house, my dad would be ticked off at the oil spots. 'Cause he got ticked off at me with my first truck."

Ty retrieved a screwdriver and proceeded to change out the license plates while Alia "assisted", which meant she watched Ty and handed him each new plate once he had removed the old one.

Chapter 19
The pink truck and Bible pizza

As much as Alia wanted to complete the beautification of her truck, the weekdays proved too busy with homework to allow time for painting. Every evening, Ty asked about her school and homework situation. Knowing that the questions would be coming deterred her from attempting any truck work during the week.

Tuesday evening, he arrived home a bit later than usual. He called Alia to come outside.

"I got you a gift." He lifted a tire and rim out of the back of his truck as the other family members trickled out to see why Ty had called for Alia. The rim matched that of three of the wheels on Alia's truck.

"Thank you! Where did you find it?"

"I went by a salvage yard in Waller and found it."

"I didn't mind the mismatched wheels, but I appreciate you for getting me a new one."

"The problem is that you don't have a spare. The mismatched wheel was probably the spare. So, if you ever got a flat or blowout, you'd be stuck."

"Then, double thank you," she said as she hugged him.

"I also checked for a tailgate, but they didn't have one for this model. Apparently, tailgates are in big demand."

"I didn't expect you to be so interested in my truck. You seemed annoyed that I even got it."

"Not annoyed. I just remember how much trouble my first truck caused me. I put in a lot of love and care on that truck. I guess it's just nostalgia." Changing the subject, he asked, "By the way, why did you choose a truck instead of a car?"

"To haul the lawnmowers."

"You still plan on mowing lawns?"

"And power washing."

"What about your job at the store?"

"I'll do that, too, but John told me how much money he got mowing lawns in the spring and summer, and I'll make more money doing that than at Bullseye, especially in the summer."

"Then you'll definitely need a tailgate to keep the mowers from falling out."

"Maybe I can borrow your tools to make one out of boards?" She phrased it as a statement but inflected it as a question.

"The way you borrowed the screwdriver?"

"You didn't *have to* install the license plates for me. I could have done them myself."

"Okay. How about I make a tailgate for you. You can be my assistant again. Maybe I'll even let you use the tools." Changing the subject again, he asked, "Does this thing have a sound system that works?"

"It's got the old small kind. You know, without a display screen. It just shows the number of the radio station. No Bluetooth or anything modern, but that's fine. It plays that radio station I like and that's all I need."

"You're still listening to that Christian station?" Sophie asked.

"Of course. Their music feels good."

Ty brought the conversation back to the truck. "Does it have a backup camera?"

"No. It's too old."

"We can buy one and put it in. Maybe John can help with that."

"I can help, too," Emi stated. "It's not just boys who can use tools."

"Do you want to mow lawns, too?" Ty asked Emi.

"Ew, no. That's too sweaty."

Sophie laughed at that statement. "I agree."

* * *

By the time Alia left for work Saturday afternoon, the truck looked entirely different. It was now a pale pink, including the wheel rims. Emi and John assisted with the paint job. At Alia's persistent questioning, each of the family members admitted that the new pink looked better than the old green and black, with its many scratches. The dents were still there, as Emi had previously pointed out, but the overall appearance looked better.

"It still looks like house paint, not the shiny auto paint," John stated.

"Say it looks better than it did," Alia insisted.

"Yes, for the third time, I agree it looks better." *Than the green and black*, he added silently. *I would have left it with the white primer.*

* * *

After church, as Alia passed Cathy Rutherford's classroom, she quickened her pace to move on without Cathy seeing her, reluctant to talk to her after ignoring her invitation last week. A few paces past the doorway, Alia stopped. Something compelled her to go back; a new thought weighing on her mind.

She walked back and stood in the doorway, not sure what to say as a greeting. When Cathy finally noticed her, Alia's words came out. "I'm coming to your pizza meeting tonight."

"That's great! I look forward to seeing you then."

What did I just do? She hadn't planned on going to Cathy's meeting, but just now committed to it. *Is this some kind of Christian mind control? Is it possible to feel anxious and compelled at the same time? Anxious about meeting strangers. Compelled that the meeting is something I'm supposed to do and will be good for me.* It felt odd and Alia couldn't figure out where the sensation came from.

* * *

Alia found four other people with Cathy Rutherford at the large round table in the back corner. Cathy sent her to order her own mini-pizza from the counter and come back.

"Sometimes we have more people," Cathy explained.

Alia had assumed there would be ten or fifteen people, but she liked the small number. Although the group size did not allow her to be anonymous, she felt more comfortable in smaller groups.

Shortly after Alia sat down at the vacant seat next to Cathy, a young girl who looked to be about six or seven years old approached Cathy and whispered in her ear.

"Not at night," Cathy said to her. "You can have Sprite or water." The girl nodded as if she expected that answer. Then she looked at Alia.

"I saw you through the window. I like your car. It's like Barbie's car."

The girl then ran to another table where a man of about thirty years old sat with a toddler.

"That's our daughter Rachel," Cathy explained. "She knows I don't let her have caffeinated drinks at night. They keep her up."

"And that's my husband and baby," said the redheaded woman seated across from Alia. She appeared to be in her late twenties. "And I want to see your Barbie car when we're done."

"For Alia's sake, let's introduce ourselves. She and I have already met, so let's start with Bobby," Cathy said, indicating the man seated next to her. He looked as if he could be a tennis pro or golf pro at a country club. Physically fit, tanned even in the winter, and wearing a Nike jacket.

"My claim to fame is being Cathy's husband and Rachel's father," he said as he took off his jacket and hung it over the back of his chair. His arms were completely covered in tattoos, shattering the country club image. "Growing up, my family went to church on Christmas and Easter. I came to Christ in prison through people who told me that God loved me despite being a troublemaker. It was a process, but here I am, twelve years later."

The restaurant staff called Alia's name to indicate her pizza was ready. The group paused while Alia retrieved her meal. Alia noted that she would need to arrive earlier next time to have her pizza ready before the meeting started.

The mother of the toddler introduced herself. "I'm Michelle Gonzales. Just call me 'Shell'. I was an atheist, raised by atheists. My husband Rick came from a Christian family, but he stopped going to church when he left for college. He never specifically abandoned God, but it just didn't matter to him. We met in college and married a couple of years later. My parents taught me that there was no god and science could explain everything. Our brains were just chemical-based computers, responding to environmental stimuli with chemical reactions that controlled our emotions and behavior.

"Then I had a baby. Phineas – Phin – is the love of my life. Well, I better say he's my co-love with Rick. Anyway, I love Phin so much, I can't believe it's nothing more than chemical reactions. I can't reconcile my atheism with my love for Phin. And Rick. So, I decided to look into Christianity, the religion of Rick's parents, but I've applied a scientific skepticism to my evaluation."

"Did you finally become a Christian?"

"I did. I learned enough to believe it's true and accepted Jesus as the one God sent to rescue me from all my bad choices. I recognize there's still a lot of stuff in the Bible that bothers me, but now I believe that just because I don't understand something, such as why God did some things or allowed some things to happen that seem to be bad things, just means that there are facts that aren't available to me. Not that the facts don't exist or never existed. That's why I come to these meetings, to see if others have already figured out about some of those things that still bother me."

The youngest of the guests, other than Alia, was the young man seated next to Shell.

"Hi, I'm Griffin. I go to Blinn College. Hoping to get into A&M in the fall. I live on campus but come back home almost every weekend because Brenham's boring. I'll head back tonight."

"Brenham? Is that where Blinn is?" Alia asked.

"Yeah. It's about a 40-minute drive."

"My doctor's in Brenham. Anyway, what brings you to these meetings?"

"Well, I was never a church person; God never mattered to me. Maybe there was a god, maybe not. If a god did exist, it didn't have any impact on the world, at least not for me. 'Jesus Christ' was just what you say when something goes wrong.

"I started going to church with my girlfriend because it was important to her. Some of the conversations with her and her dad got me thinking that maybe there was something to God and I should check it out. She introduced me to Cathy, who introduced me to this group."

"Doesn't your girlfriend come with you?"

"We broke up a few months ago, so she stopped coming. I think I was a little too slow on this Christian journey. I'd stopped coming to these meetings. Anyway, she didn't need this kind of discussion, she's already got it all figured out. After a while, though, I felt like I was missing something, so I started coming again this year. It was my new year's resolution."

The twenty-something man with the olive complexion introduced himself. "I'm Shakir Mansour. I teach middle school math and I started coming here because I'm a rude Muslim who was forced to confront his own biases," he chuckled. "I constantly challenged my Christian friends in their beliefs to show them that Christianity was false. Most of them didn't know squat about their own religion, so it was easy to argue them into a corner."

"Did you convert anyone to Islam?" Alia asked.

"No one. They mostly thought I was being rude. Most American Christians don't feel the need to learn the deep truths that are the foundation of their religion because they're never challenged like I was challenging them. They just carry on with the beliefs that their parents or grandparents had.

"Many Muslims in Muslim-majority countries are the same way. It was like I was wrestling children, and then congratulating myself for winning. I'm lucky my closest Christian friends didn't abandon me for my rudeness.

"Then one day, one of them brought a friend to one of our pickup basketball games, and this guy knew a lot. When they mentioned church, I started my usual ragging on Christianity and this guy had an answer for everything. It turned out that his family were Christians in Iran and, being from a Muslim country, they had to have a deep understanding of Christianity to resist the beliefs and harassment of their Muslim neighbors. In that battle, I became the child. Then he challenged me to examine Islam as critically as I did Christianity. That effort required me to research more into Islam and I found my resolve weakening. I'm pissed that the imams gave me incomplete answers. It's like they don't even know the answers themselves. One of my friends introduced me to this group – I call it 'Bible pizza' – and I've been coming for a few months."

"But you haven't converted yet?"

"If I was a complete outsider, looking at Islam and Christianity with equal criticism and skepticism, I'd probably pick Christianity. In fact, I know I would, but it's hard to abandon everything I grew up with. There's a lot of cultural heritage that comes along with it."

"Are your parents mad at you? Like, will they disown you if you convert?"

"Oh, yeah. My parents are very upset that I've been asking these questions, but they've also heard the sorry answers that the imams give and sympathize with my frustration at not getting direct answers. I've discussed the results of my research with them. I don't think they'll disown me, but they won't be happy. I suspect that if I do convert, my little sister will, too. I sort of feel sorry for my parents. They don't have the social connections outside of Islam that my sister and I have. But my relatives in Egypt would probably disown me."

Alia's turn was next and she decided to give them a summarized version of her situation. "My name is Alia. I guess you know that already. I come from a Muslim family, too. I had doubts even in elementary school. I didn't understand why my family had these religious rules that made us so different from my school friends. When I questioned it, my parents just said it's Allah's will. As I got older, I would ask more specific questions and they still couldn't give me good answers. So, I started realizing they didn't know why we did what we did, like dressing a certain way or avoiding certain foods. No one knew. At least that's how it seemed to me. I got the idea that everyone's just pretending it's real so they can continue the social life, like an extreme fantasy fan club."

"That's an interesting way to put it," Shakir said.

"That's how I saw it. So I started rebelling. My father didn't take it very well. He is very committed to Islam. Eventually, I ran away and got into some bad stuff. Anyway, I ended up living with a family that goes to Cathy's church. I started going to church with them out of boredom and curiosity and I started listening to a Christian radio station. I felt like I was in a dark place, and the music and church shine a light that gives me hope. I want it to be real, but I'm afraid one day I'll find out it's just a different fantasy fan club, like changing from a Harry Potter fan club to a Star Wars fan club. That I'll find some big flaw that will show it's all fake." She looked down at her plate, unsure how to end the explanation

"Thank you, Alia," Bobby said. "We want to bring those difficult questions out in the open and try our best to answer them. The Bible is our guide. If there are questions out there in pop culture about Jesus or Christianity, we first look to the Bible for answers. That's where it gets harder. Sometimes the Biblical answer isn't straightforward and we have to look for context in sources outside of the Bible. We don't always have a ready answer, but we're not going to shy away from the question.

"Alia, the rules we follow for evaluating a passage of scripture from the Bible are, one, restate the passage in your own words; two, say what you like about the passage; three, say what you don't like about the passage, what bothers you about it; and four, feel free to eat while others are talking." Bobby pushed his plate forward and set his Bible on the table.

"I think the rule about eating should be first," Griffin stated, taking a bite of his pizza.

"I'll keep that in mind next time," Bobby chuckled. "Shell, why don't you start us off with one of the areas that bother you."

Chapter 20
Modifications

Alia spent the next few days coming up with designs for the last stage of her truck beautification project. By Thursday evening, she had determined the final design and even made a few pencil marks on the pink paint before sunset. Before rearranging the vehicles so that Sophie could pull her car into the garage, Sophie's study group friends walked up to see Alia's masterpiece in progress. She showed them photos on her phone of the truck in its ugly phase, for contrast.

"Do you like it?" she asked the group.

Whether they did or not, they all agreed that it was a huge improvement over its previous condition. Sophie had warned them ahead of time of Alia's continuous requests of acceptance for the truck. Usually reserved with her demeanor, Alia talked excitedly about the purchase, learning to drive a manual transmission, and her vision for the detailed artwork. The pencil marks weren't readily visible in the dim evening light, but Alia made sure to point them out while explaining her vision of the finished masterpiece.

"Hey, maybe I should do something like that with my car," one of the girls commented. "It looks almost as bad as your truck did. It's been handed down from my uncle to my brother to me. And it was already used when my uncle got it."

"Yeah, that time I rode with you to lunch, I was scared stuff was gonna fall off," another stated.

"I can't wait to see it in full daylight when you're done, Alia."

"It should be done this weekend."

"Sophie, you have to invite us back when it's daylight."

"Next week, I'm coming over earlier. I'm not waiting for Sophie to get out of her class," another said.

"How do you know we're having a study sleepover next week?" Sophie asked.

"'Cause I just made an executive decision."

* * *

When the study group returned the next Thursday, black swirl patterns reminiscent of curving vines covered the pink truck. The patterns made the dents less obvious.

Neighbors who hadn't spoken to Alia before had come over late Sunday afternoon to see her "art car" as she applied the finishing touches. Even Emi had John record a video of a walk around the truck, while Emi stood in the truck bed describing the painting process and pointing out Alia as the artist. Emi posted the video to her Jentler Hair YouTube channel, despite it having nothing to do with hair.

* * *

In early February, a package showed up at the door with Ty's name on it. When he got home, he handed it to Alia.

"Another present for you."

She opened the package to find a backup camera kit inside.

"Cool! But I've gotten the hang of just using the mirrors now."

"Not according to the tracks in the grass at the end of the driveway. Besides this will make it easier to back into parking spaces."

"Thank you. Can we put it in this weekend?"

Before Ty could answer, John and Lizzie arrived and headed straight for the open box that Ty and Alia were examining. Except that Lizzie made a slight detour to a shelf in the living room to grab a teddy bear and place it on the mantle with the five other bears. Then she arrived at the kitchen table to see the open box.

"Hi, Alia. Hi Ty. I love to get packages. Mom does all her shopping online now, so we're always getting stuff delivered. I get all excited about some new thing arriving, and when I open it, I find it's soap or something." Lizzie leaned forward, in between Ty and Alia. "What'd you get?"

Lizzie held up the backup camera box.

"Oh. Is that for your truck? Did its camera break?"

"It didn't have one."

"Really? I thought all cars had backup cameras."

"I did, too, but it's too old. Ty's gonna help me set it up on Saturday." Ty looked at her and smiled. She had asked, but he hadn't answered before they were distracted by John and Lizzie's arrival.

"John, you were good at fixing lawnmowers," Lizzie stated. "Why don't you help her?"

"I don't think cameras are anything like lawnmowers, but sure, I'll help."

"Sorry, Ty, but you and I can still work on the tailgate later," Alia offered as if replacing him for the camera installation meant he lost a coveted privilege.

"I'm fine with John handling the camera. I have a few handyman tasks I need to do Saturday, anyway."

John and Lizzie went upstairs and disappeared into the upstairs den.

Emi went to the mantle and picked up the teddy bear Lizzie had placed there and returned it to its place on the shelf. She stood back and stared at the bear for a moment. "Well, she is here all the time," Emi muttered to herself. She picked up the bear and put it back on the mantle.

* * *

Alia and John sat in the front seat of the truck with their heads nearly touching as they watched a video on John's phone of someone installing a similar camera on a vehicle.

"This is how I learned how to fix the lawnmower. I just watched videos." He stopped the video. "We have to get the video cable from the camera at the back all the way to the inside of the cab to the video monitor. It says there is a hole for other wires to enter the cab, so if we find that hole, we can push the camera cable through there."

John leaned over with his head nearly in Alia's lap as he tried to look under the dashboard to find where other wires and cables came in. Alia scooted over and got out, squatting down on the pavement and peering under the dashboard to see what John saw. She leaned in so that her long hair fell into John's face, blocking his view.

Pushing her hair aside, he said, "It's right there," pointing.

"I'll push the cable through and you pull it from underneath," Alia stated.

John spent much of the installation process on his back underneath the truck, or at least, with his head under the truck. He strung the cable along the undercarriage and looked for places to attach the cable so it didn't hang down. Periodically John held his hand out and Alia placed a zip tie in it. More than once, John accidentally closed his hand around Alia's hand, not just the zip tie. From his position, he couldn't see Alia smile slightly each time he did that.

"The video cable is done. What's next?" John asked.

"We need to connect the power wires. According to the video, the red wire needs to connect to the wire for the backup lights."

After figuring out which of the wires exiting the taillight assembly went to the backup light, John repositioned himself under the back of the truck, looking up at the wires.

211

"I see the wire we need to splice into. There's another wire under here that looks frayed. It looks like it's been rubbing against something. I think we need to replace it before we do anything with the camera."

"What does it go to?"

"I can't tell. Maybe the brake lights."

Alia crawled under the truck next to John to see for herself. "Show me," she said, her voice seeming to be right next to his ear. John turned his head towards her, to find her face less than an inch from his.

"Show me the wire."

He scooted over a bit so that she could get close enough to see it. She scooted over, too.

"I don't see it."

With the hand closest to the taillight, John pointed a flashlight towards the frayed wire. With the hand closest to Alia, he grabbed her hand, folding all but her forefinger down, and guided her finger to touch the frayed spot. "See it now?"

"Yes. Thanks." Again, her voice sounded right next to his ear.

John turned his head to see her face and his lips accidentally brushed against hers. "Sorry!"

"It's okay. I won't tell Lizzie," she giggled. "After all, it's not like the New Year's Eve kiss."

"Hey, that one was because I didn't understand the plan."

"You're still holding my hand."

"Oh," he said, releasing his grip.

* * *

The Saturday before Valentine's Day, Alia had a dinner date with Andy. She had mixed feelings about the relationship although she enjoyed their time together; Andy was fun to hang with, if a bit too talkative. So far, their time together was somewhat like brother and sister. At least it was to Alia. A Valentine's date may require a reevaluation of the relationship.

Andy texted his arrival from the driveway before walking up to the door to ring the bell. He held a bouquet of flowers. A little burst of insecurity flashed through her mind. *Am I obligated to tell him I don't have romantic feelings for him? I didn't have them for my first boyfriend either. So why did I have them for Caleb when we didn't even know each other that well? Everyone knows how that turned out.*

Alia couldn't bring herself to tell him she didn't have a romantic interest in him, especially when the first words out of his mouth were, "I love what you've done with your truck!"

Before she could even respond, he commanded, "Show me up close," as he started walking back down the walkway to the truck parked in the street. He still held the flowers. "This is awesome! Seeing it up close is much better than in the pictures. And you don't even notice the dents." He pointed toward the truck with the flowers before remembering he was holding them. "Oh. These are for you," he said holding them out to Alia.

As she took the flowers, Andy asked, "Do people stop you to ask about it?"

Without realizing it, she was talking more than Andy as she explained the reactions of neighbors, classmates, and random strangers in parking lots. When she talked about a subject that she was passionate about, she could be every bit as talkative as Andy. It just didn't happen often.

After their dinner, coffee, and a walk around the man-made lake between the restaurant complex and the nearby neighborhood, Andy drove them back to the Jensen house. The walk wasn't quite as long as Andy had hoped as their light jackets didn't offer enough warmth from the frigid air and they both wanted to get back to the car's heater. They ended their previous outings – Alia was reluctant to call them dates – with a brief hug outside the front door. Tonight as they embraced, Andy didn't let go after the standard three seconds. Neither did Alia. It had been a long time since she had experienced a full, lasting hug from someone close to her. She hadn't realized how much she needed it and the warm, comforting feeling surprised her. The annoying clown had become a good friend. Just a friend?

She opened her eyes, not realizing she had closed them, then released her arms and pulled back slightly, which Andy took as the signal to do the same. However, Alia didn't pull away completely. She pulled away enough to look into his eyes. Then she closed her eyes again and kissed him quickly.

"Call me tomorrow," she whispered, before opening the door and disappearing into the house.

* * *

On Valentine's Day itself, John normally would have gone to Lizzie's house to pick her up for a romantic dinner, but she insisted on meeting him at his house. After quickly greeting John, she sought out Alia.

Lizzie sported a very different look than on other days. She let her hair down, wore contact lens instead of her usual glasses, and had on a "date" dress.

"Wow, I almost didn't recognize you. You look amazing!" Alia expressed upon seeing her.

"Thank you. I usually have to dress down so I don't distract all the boys. I just wouldn't have time for all of them."

"Hey!" John exclaimed.

"Aw," she said, hugging him, "you're the exception. I always have time for you."

Looking back at Alia, Lizzie said, "Here," holding out a greeting card to Alia. "Happy Valentine's Day."

"Thank you, but I don't understand," Alia replied, puzzled. "Valentine's Day is for romantics, not friends."

"Sometimes friends are who you need at the moment."

Alia removed the card from the envelope.

Someday you'll find that perfect someone.
Until then, you have friends who love you.

On behalf of your future sweetheart,
Happy Valentine's Day.

Love, Lizzie

"Thank you," Alia responded. "Sometimes I have a hard time knowing what love really means. I'm still figuring it out."

* * *

School had become enough of a routine that Alia – and Ty – felt comfortable adding an extra shift at the department store during the week without jeopardizing her grades. Since she had completed the truck beautification project, she could use the newly freed-up hours on Saturdays to make up any homework delayed by the weekday work shift.

On those days when the homework level seemed stressful, she would make time to visit Bob Barker. Ty and Sophie found it odd that taking time away from homework for dog cuddles could make the remaining time more efficient. Nevertheless, it seemed to work.

Alia reminded Ty that spring was approaching and she needed a tailgate for the truck to keep her lawn equipment from falling out. Thus, one of those recently freed-up Saturday mornings became another truck project morning. While John and Emi slept in, Alia had no trouble waking up early to resume work on her truck.

After taking careful measurements of the rear opening of the truck bed, Ty had Alia drive him to the hardware store for square steel tubing and other supplies, then on to Hockley Industrial Machines, where he worked Monday through Friday.

Carrying some of the hardware supplies, he showed her the factory floor before taking her to a work area fitted with cutting tools and welding equipment. After they both donned safety goggles, Alia watched as Ty cut the square tubing to the precise lengths. Using a drill press, he drilled holes at carefully marked points in the pieces that would become the right and left vertical supports. Once the cutting and drilling were done, they switched out the safety goggles for welding helmets. Ty welded the pieces together into a ladder pattern. The finished product became the tailgate frame.

"Do you have any girl welders here?"

"A couple, but it's mostly men."

"Does it pay well?"

"Probably more than most college graduates get when they first graduate, especially if they have to make student loan payments."

"Does this company train people how to do it?"

"No. You have to get trained first."

"Can you teach me?"

"I can teach the basics, but Lone Star College has classes that would probably do a better job than I could. That's where I got certified for some advanced techniques."

"You can get a college degree in welding?"

"No, but you can get certificates in different types of welding." He paused, remembering something. "I take that back. There *is* a college degree in Applied Science that includes welding, but that means having to take other classes that have nothing to do with welding, like history, computers, and art.

You can start working after just getting the certificates. You don't necessarily have to get a degree."

"I've got to think about this."

Back at the house, Ty and Alia added the additional hardware to attach the tailgate to the truck and be able to lock and release the gate. Finally, Ty showed Alia how to use his table saw and directed her in cutting the wood planks that would cover the inside and outside of the gate. Dealing with the wooden pieces was all Alia's effort, with direction from Ty.

During the earlier trip to the hardware store, Ty bought extra boards that Alia could use as ramps to get her mower and power washer in and out of the truck.

Once again, Alia called the family members out to view her handiwork. "Look what we made," she said excitedly pointing to the tailgate.

Sunday Alia painted it with white primer.

* * *

At the Sunday night meeting at Paolo's Pizza, Alia brought up the first topic. "I've been reading the Jesus parts of the Bible and I want to know why Jesus refers to himself as the 'son of man' instead of 'son of god'. Don't Christians believe he's the son of God?"

"Shakir, do you want to take this one?" Bobby asked. "We covered this a few weeks ago for Shakir," he explained.

"Sure," Shakir replied to Bobby's question. "The phrase 'son of god' didn't have the same meaning to the people of

Jesus' time as it does now. To them, it just meant someone who believed in God and followed his commands. So, basically, any devout Jewish man back then was a son of God, but the term 'son of man' meant something else entirely. Today, we might interpret it as meaning 'I'm just a human,' which is an odd phrase to call yourself. 'Look, regular human me will be betrayed.' The phrase just doesn't make sense. However, to the people of Jesus' time, it referred to a vision by the prophet Daniel. Daniel saw a man in heaven seated at the right hand of God who had authority over everything and was worshipped, and Daniel referred to him as 'son of man'. So when Jesus called himself that, he meant he was the heavenly person at God's right hand."

"It's easy to miss that significance," Shell interjected. "Except when the Gospels tell how the Jewish leaders reacted when they heard Jesus call himself that. By their reaction, we know that title is controversial for them. They acted like it was blasphemy."

"Does that make sense?" Cathy asked Alia, who nodded in affirmation.

"Who has the next topic?" Bobby asked.

* * *

Monday Alia finished the tailgate with pink paint before Ty got home to ask her about homework.

* * *

Ty hung another photo on the staircase wall. Actually, it included two photos within one frame. One photo showed Alia's truck before her renovations. The other showed the painted version with a proud Alia standing next to it. Ty made sure the angle of that photo showed the tailgate.

Chapter 21
Spring break anniversary

Spring break meant different things to different people. For the family's college friends, it meant vacations to beach towns. For the teens, it meant a welcomed break from schoolwork. For Alia, it meant opportunities to earn more money from lawn care, pressure washing, and working additional shifts at the department store. For Sophie and Ty, it meant a wedding anniversary.

Ty and Sophie booked a room at the Hotel Galvez in Galveston for Saturday night at the start of spring break. They planned to drive down Saturday morning and arrive in time for brunch. Emi and John, and certainly Alia, were old enough to take care of themselves for the weekend, and Ty and Sophie trusted them not to throw a wild party while they were gone. Besides, Ty told them his parents might stop by to check on them. Though, he had failed to mention that to his parents.

Even before Ty and Sophie left the house, Alia and John had left for their respective projects. John had several lawns to mow and Alia had a large pressure washing job: a neighbor's pool deck and driveway.

Alia started on the pool deck. When she began the job, the brisk morning air required that she wear a waterproof jacket. She had considered wearing jeans or leggings but thought once they got wet, they wouldn't provide much warmth. Sports shorts would be fine, she thought, and she expected the temperature to become more tolerable during the job.

* * *

Sophie and Ty arrived at the Hotel Galvez in time for brunch, well before the check-in time for their room. They stored their overnight bags with the concierge before heading to the hotel restaurant. They passed a few college spring breakers in the lobby. Sophie, in her Prairie View A&M jersey, fit right in.

As they waited to be seated, a preteen girl with multiple braids pointed at them and spoke excitedly to her parents. She looked up something on her phone and held it up to them to see. The father shrugged his shoulders while the mother nodded towards Ty and Sophie, now seated at a table.

The girl and her mother approached Ty. "Are you Emi's dad?" she asked.

"Um, sort of. She's my sister-in-law."

"And you do her hair, right?"

"Yeah," he replied, drawing out the word, puzzled. "Do you go to school with Emi?"

"No, but I watch her videos. I thought it was you, and when I saw her Prairie View shirt," she said, pointing to Sophie. "I knew it had to be you; 'cause one of the videos had another girl with that shirt. I love when you do Emi's hair. The way you get along is fun and… um," she paused as if searching for the right word. "…Happy. Fun and happy."

"I'm Ty and this is my wife – Emi's sister – Sophie. What's your name?"

"Jasmine. This is my mom, and my dad's over there," she said, pointing.

"After watching your videos, Jasmine started pestering her dad to do her hair," Jasmine's mother explained. "He's tried a few times, but I don't think he's as happy about the videos as she is. That's why he's standing back there."

When Jasmine and her mother returned to join her father at their own table, Sophie started laughing. "You're a celebrity! I thought she was going to ask for an autograph."

A few minutes later, another family joined Jasmine's family. They also had a daughter who looked about Jasmine's age. After a few minutes of discussion and views on their phones, both girls approached Ty.

"Can we get a selfie with you?"

Sophie poked Ty's leg under the table.

* * *

By mid-morning the sun had heated the air enough that it felt quite warm. Alia shed the windbreaker. Once the pool deck was dirt-free, she disconnected the water hose and rolled the pressure washer out of the backyard to reconnect the hose to a faucet near the driveway. The lack of shade over the driveway added to the heat. She removed her shirt to cool off, revealing a bikini top.

* * *

Ty and Sophie took a stroll along the beach after brunch. Although the sun hung high in the sky, the gulf breeze provided a pleasant temperature. Groups of college students were clustered in various spots along the beach and at the shops across from it. Many were in swimsuits, but a few wore their school jerseys. U of H, TSU, Texas A&M, and Prairie View were represented. Sophie got a shout-out from a cluster of Prairie View students.

"Do you want to join them?" Ty asked.

"I don't recognize anyone in that group. They're just cheering for my shirt."

A few steps later, Sophie heard someone calling her name. She looked around to see a group waving at her from a gift shop.

"See, you have fans, too," Ty teased.

As they walked over to the waving students, Sophie recognized her school friends. Ty also recognized two from the study sleepovers: Toni and Alayna. He didn't know the other girl or the three guys.

"Sophie, I thought you weren't doing spring break. Did hubby let you out?" Toni asked.

"This 'hubby' is not holding her prisoner," Ty said with faux indignation.

"Then y'all come hang with us."

"I don't want you to miss out on the full college experience, which includes spring break," Ty stated, before adding, "At least for a day or two, not the whole week."

"But this is our anniversary. We're here to celebrate each other." Sophie pointed out.

"We can celebrate each other all night," Ty countered, raising his eyebrows up and down, bringing smiles to the other students. Then he leaned in a whispered into her ear, "And we can 'celebrate' this afternoon when our room is ready."

"Okay. We'll hang with y'all until our room is ready. Then we plan to hang out by the pool."

"Where're y'all staying?" Toni asked.

"The Galvez," Sophie said, pointing to it.

"Us, too! We'll do some pool time with you."

"Just so you understand, it may take us a while to change into swimsuits," Ty said with a wink.

"Yeah, I know how that is," said one of the guys, raising his hand in a high-five position to Ty. Ty smiled and slapped his hand in returning the salute. "Anniversary," he said knowingly to the girl next to him.

"Yeah. Anniversary, not monthiversary, Kellen."

* * *

After loading the equipment into the back of the pink truck, Alia dried herself off with a towel. The towel felt a bit more scratchy than she remembered, especially when she applied pressure to remove the splatters of mud from her legs.

At home, she jumped in the shower to remove all the remaining dirt. Although the shower was set at her usual temperature, the spray felt like boiling water against her skin. She let out a yelp and immediately turned the water to cold. Only then did she realize that not only did she have a sunburn, but the extent of it. The contrast was extreme between the exposed areas and those covered by sneakers, shorts, and the bikini top. She carefully rinsed off and turned off the shower. The towel against her sunburnt skin stung like fire. She wiped the white areas and decided everything else could air dry, holding her arms out away from her sides.

* * *

Sophie and Ty finished their afternoon celebration of each other in the hotel room and proceeded to get ready for the pool. As Sophie began to put on her swimsuit, Ty reminded, "Sunscreen."

He squirted out a large dollop of sunscreen on his hands and began applying it to Sophie's back. With her backside completed, he stepped closer and wrapped his arms around her in a hug from behind, pressing her lotioned back against his chest. Ty squirted more sunscreen on his hands and began rubbing it onto his wife's front side.

Sophie smiled broadly, not that Ty could see. "I thought we were finished playing," she said.

"I'm just applying the sunscreen," he said seriously.

"I love you."

"I love you, too."

They exited the hotel room just as Sophie's friends were coming out of their room across the hall.

"I didn't know you were on our floor," Alayna said.

"What a surprise," Sophie replied without enthusiasm. She put her mouth close to Ty's ear, "I'm glad they're not in the room next door."

* * *

Alia heard the back door slam and could tell from the footsteps that it was John, arriving home from mowing lawns, or as he liked to call it, "making money." He called out "Hey!"

"Hi!" Alia called back from the doorway of her room. "Do you have anything for sunburn? Like lotion or something?"

"I think we have some aloe gel if Ty didn't take it with him." After a couple of minutes of cabinet doors slamming, he called out, "Found it!"

While John rummaged through cabinets for the aloe gel, Alia put on shorts. She attempted to put on a bra, but its shape didn't match that of the bikini top, and the places where it touched the sunburn stung. She put the bra back in the drawer.

John found her standing at the sink area of her bathroom, with her back towards the doorway, arms held out away from her sides, and wearing nothing but shorts. Her back was bright red.

"Dang! That's bad! I'm not sure we have enough gel." When he approached closer, he saw her full glory in the reflection of the mirror. He took a step back and held out the bottle. "Here."

"Can you do it? I can't reach my back and it hurts just to bend my arms."

He glanced at the mirror again and imagined Lizzie looking over his shoulder wagging her finger. "Maybe you should get Emi."

"She's not here. Please. It hurts."

"I'll start on your back." He concentrated on the task at hand and tried to avoid looking in the mirror again.

"We're gonna run out of gel. I'm calling Emi to borrow some from the Butlers. I think they buy it by the case since Anna has the whitest skin of anyone I know." Emi had been hanging out with friends on the street and agreed to break away for the assignment.

After Alia's neck and back were gelled up, John squatted down to do the backs of her legs.

"Okay. Everything in back is done," he said, standing.

She turned around to face him. John's eyes widened and his mouth gaped open as he audibly sucked in air. The white of the two non-burnt areas appeared to glow in contrast to the red everywhere else.

"What? Is it worse in front?"

"No. It's just as sunburned as the back."

"Is there any gel left?"

"A little."

"Go ahead."

He squatted down again and devoted his attention to the fronts of her legs. *Don't look up. Don't look up.*

* * *

Sophie lay on a lounge chair next to Toni, sucking on a piña colada, while Ty lounged on Sophie's other side with a margarita. Toni looked around at the numerous guests around the pool and got Sophie's attention.

"You're not jealous of Ty being around all these half-naked college girls?"

"We had the same problem on our honeymoon last year. The cruise ship was full of spring breakers."

Overhearing the conversation, Ty pointed out, "You did a pretty good job of keeping me from noticing." He held the margarita straw over her chest and playfully shook it so a few drops of cold liquid dripped down, startling her with its coolness.

"Trade." She reached out her hand and he passed over the margarita as she handed over her piña colada. She resumed the conversation. "Except that time we accidentally came across the girls sunbathing topless on the upper deck."

"Oh?" chuckled Toni. "Did he have roaming eyes?"

"Hey, I love my wife, but I'm still a man, and there were boobs everywhere."

"We backed right out of there and I dragged him straight back to our cabin."

"Was that like a time out?" Toni asked, laughing.

"No. It was heaven," Ty replied. "Now hand back my margarita," he commanded Sophie.

"Hey, how come Sophie can get alcohol, and we can't?" Sean questioned, finally realizing the beverage situation.

Sophie held up her left hand and wiggled her ring finger. "Spouse privilege."

* * *

Emi came running up the stairs with the bottle of aloe gel to see John and Alia in the bathroom, with John kneeling before a seemingly naked Alia.

"JOHN!" Emi screamed. "What the heck are you doing?!"

"She's sunburned pretty bad."

Emi pushed John hard enough to topple him over. "Go!" Emi commanded. "Get out!"

As soon as John left Emi turned back to Alia and slapped her across a sunburned thigh.

"Oww! That hurts so bad! Why'd you do that?"

"You can't have John. He has a girlfriend and I like her."

"He's just helping me with the sunburn. And I like Lizzie, too."

"Did he 'help' with that part yet?" Emi asked, pointing to her bare chest.

"No. We ran out of gel."

"Good." Emi held out the bottle. "Do it yourself."

"I'm not trying to steal John away from Lizzie. I swear."

"Yeah, well it's not helping when you're flaunting your naked body around him. Keep your clothes on around other people. You're not a prostitute anymore."

Between the pain of the sunburn and the sting of Emi's words, Alia felt like crying. She grabbed a towel and held it up to her chest. Tears welled up in her eyes.

"It's not like that. It hurts so much I can't even think about... about that kind of stuff. I tried to put on a bra, but it rubs the sunburn and hurts."

Emi stared at Alia's face in skepticism before walking through the bathroom to her own room. She returned a minute later with silk pajamas. "Wear these. They'll feel smoother against your skin than a T-shirt. I'll get you some Tylenol." As Emi went downstairs, she added, "When it's time to reapply the gel to your back, call *me*. Not John. Everything else you can do yourself."

* * *

Late in the evening, Sophie and Ty were back in their room enjoying another intimate moment of personal 'celebration' when they heard pounding on the door.

"Sophie! Sophie's hubby! We're going dancing! Come with us!"

"Can't I have some private time with my wife?!" Ty shouted back.

"Can we watch?!" came a masculine reply through the door.

"NO!" Ty and Sophie both replied at once.

About an hour later, there came another pounding at the door. "Sophie! It's Toni. Can I come in?"

"I thought you went dancing!" Sophie called back from the bed, reluctant to move out of her comfortable cuddle position.

"They wouldn't let us in the club. Said it was too crowded. And now Alayna and Jeffrey locked me out."

"Did y'all get in a fight?"

"No. They're... uh... busy. With each other. Can I stay with you?"

"Enjoying spring break?" Ty asked Sophie in a whisper. She frowned and made a growling sound. He got up to get dressed. "Go ahead and let her in," he said, picking up her discarded T-shirt from the floor and tossing it to her.

* * *

In the morning, Ty awakened on the floor between Sophie's side of the bed and the wall for the bathroom. He had arranged their clothes and extra towels on the floor as a makeshift bed for himself. Fortunately, the actual bed came with extra pillows that he used for his head. While his body ached from sleeping on the hard floor, Toni and Sophie looked comfortable on the king-size bed.

* * *

Lizzie returned from a family ski trip with a goggle tan and Andy came back from his own spring break beach trip with bright red skin. By Friday, Alia's skin had already blistered and started to peel. The Jensen/Butler family left for an overnight trip to San Antonio to escort Anna back to school at the University of Texas-San Antonio and spend a day at Six Flags Fiesta Texas.

"Who's riding with me and who's riding with Ty?" Anna asked as the Jensen household members were loading bags into the Escalade. She had walked down from her house to find passengers to make the drive more interesting.

"You," Sophie stated.

"I'll go with you, too," Alia added.

"Aw, my own wife's abandoning me?" Ty asked.

"I see you every day. I don't get to see my best friend that often anymore."

"I thought I was your best friend," Ty stated.

"I don't get to see my *first* best friend that often anymore," Sophie corrected.

Ty moved on to another subject. "Alia, what's with the pajama pants?"

"They're not pajamas. They're just very loose pants to cover my legs. I can't take any more sunburns."

"I guess that explains the long sleeve shirt, too."

"You just need a friend to help you put sunscreen on the hard-to-reach places," Anna commented to Alia while winking at John.

"Or a husband," Sophie whispered to Ty.

"Don't tell her that!" Emi exclaimed to Anna. "She...." Her voice trailed off. She sighed as she looked from Anna to John and back to Anna. "Nevermind."

"Did I miss something?" Anna asked.

"Whatever it was, I missed it too," Sophie said.

"Ne-ver-mind," Emi said again, enunciating each syllable. Changing the subject, she asked, "What are we doing for lunch?"

"I thought we could have lunch at that place on the River Walk that you liked so much last time," Ty answered.

"Only if we eat indoors," Emi responded. As the family started laughing, Emi added, "Alia needs more time to recover from her sunburn."

John whispered to Alia, "Emi has a phobia about pigeons."

Chapter 22
Proof of life

Alia climbed into her truck after the Sunday night meeting at Paolo's Pizza and started the engine. On the dashboard, the check engine light appeared. She might not have noticed the light, except that the engine started making an unusual rumbling noise. She flagged down Griffin as he climbed into his car.

When he walked over, she explained, "My engine doesn't sound right and there's a weird light on the dash. Do you know what's wrong with it?"

Griffin looked inside at the warning lights on the dash. "That's the check engine light. It means the truck's computer recognizes something's wrong. It could be something like a bad sparkplug or a problem with the valves. I don't know enough about engines to tell what's wrong. You'd better take it to a shop."

"Do you think it'll be safe to drive it tonight?"

"I can follow you home in case it breaks down on the way."

"Thank you. Let me call Ty before we go to let him know the situation."

"Is that your host dad?"

She smiled. "Host? I guess so, but he's not nearly old enough to be my dad."

After a brief discussion with Ty, she reported back to Griffin. "Ty told me to take it straight to a repair shop by our house. He can meet me there."

"Or I can take you home."

Alia had another conversation with Ty. She looked back at Griffin. "You can take me home."

"Give me your phone number. Let's keep an open line in case your truck gets worse. You can tell me and we can pull over."

During the drive, Alia learned about Griffin, Blinn College, and the Blue Bell ice cream factory in Brenham. Griffin learned about Alia's catching up on school she had missed, her jobs in lawn care and at Bullseye, and that she maybe had a boyfriend, but wasn't sure of the relationship.

"I liked how Shakir said that God went out of his way to reach out to the screw-ups of the world," Alia stated into her phone on the drive. "I'd kind of heard about the prodigal son story before, but not the details. Like, that the rich father ran down the street to hug his screwed-up son who'd wasted his life and the father threw a big party to welcome him back. It fits with the theme of one of my favorite songs, where it says God will send out an army to rescue you, but the song doesn't say the person who is getting rescued caused her own problems. So, it's nice to think God will rescue a screw-up if they show that they want to be rescued. Like in the song, it says God hears your S-O-S."

"Yeah. I don't think of myself as a screw-up, but I've done some screwed-up things, so it's good to know God will take you back. And Shell's funny," Griffin stated, seeming to move on. "When Cathy brought up Hosea and how God told him to marry a promiscuous wife, and you asked what promiscuous meant…"

"Well, it's not a word I hear every day," Alia interrupted, somewhat embarrassed at not knowing the meaning.

"I'm not criticizing you, I just meant Shell's explanation was hilarious. There we were, talking about the Bible and church stuff, and Shell just came out and said, 'God told Hosea to marry a slut.' I couldn't help but laugh. I just imagined little old church ladies having to explain that in Sunday School."

"I guess it *is* pretty funny. I just don't really know what's normal for church. It's very different from the *masjid* I went to. People at church sing and seem happy. So, if the preacher started talking about sluts, I'd just assume it's normal. By the way, we're almost at the auto shop."

Alia thought about that story. God directed the prophet Hosea to marry a slut – Shell's description – as an example of God's relationship with "his people". When Hosea's wife tramped around – again, Shell's description – God directed Hosea to get her back, even going so far as to pay off her debt to get her back. The group speculated what kind of debt she had, but Alia thought it was obvious. A prostitute wanting to get out of the business had to pay an exit fee, a price too high for her to pay on her own. As soon as Alia said it, she feared someone would ask her how she knew that. However, before anyone had a chance to ask, Cathy moved on to explain that the bizarre story demonstrated how God always took his people back after they strayed. It was about a relationship, not about following rules.

"I felt sorry for Hosea," Griffin stated. "It seemed kinda cruel that God would make him marry someone who 'tramped around', as Shell put it."

"Yeah, I felt that way, too, but maybe that's one of those cases where we don't have all the facts. Maybe Hosea was determined to get married and was trying to decide who to marry and had two toxic women in mind. Like, maybe God already told him not to marry either one and he was, like, determined to pick one. Or maybe God wanted him to marry an ugly girl and Hosea refused. So God said, 'Fine, if you're not gonna listen to me about who I wanted you to marry, then out of your own two choices, go ahead and marry Gomer, the beautiful slut.'"

"I think the name Gomer should have been a deterrent," Griffin stated.

"I thought the same thing!" Alia laughed.

Alia pulled into the auto repair shop parking lot and backed into a space directly across from one of the garage doors. Griffin pulled up and stopped his car in front of her truck. Alia disconnected their call and texted Ty to announce she was now leaving the auto shop with Griffin and would be home shortly.

As Alia was getting out of Griffin's car at the house, Griffin said, "I'm sorry about your truck. I hope it doesn't cost much to fix, but I'm not sorry I got your phone number."

"You could have just asked."

* * *

"Ty and Sophie said they'd cover the repairs, but I feel bad about that," Alia told Griffin via FaceTime on Monday evening. "They're already paying everything else for me, and this is a lot of money. One part of me thinks I made a mistake buying that truck and I should just have it towed to a junkyard, but another part of me says I can't abandon it. Like it's a person and it deserves to be loved. And I put a lot of effort into making it look nice."

"You can't give it up. Maybe just let it sit until you earn enough money to have it fixed."

"Without the truck, I can't get to some of the lawn mowing customers. I can get John to do those, but then it'll take longer for me to earn the money. Then there's the problem of getting to and from school."

"Did your grandparents ever give you money for birthdays or Christmas?"

"Birthdays, yes. Christmas, no. Christmas wasn't much of a thing at my house. Anyway, I don't have access to the money."

"Did you keep it in a box or something at your house?"

"No, my parents put it in a savings account for me." As the words left her mouth, she realized what she just said. Somewhere there was a bank account with her name on it.

"Which bank?" Griffin asked.

"I don't remember," she lamented. "I can picture where it is, but I don't remember the bank's name."

As he talked to Alia, Griffin opened the map application on his computer. "Near your parents' house?"

"Yes. In St. Louis."

"Is that where you used to live?"

"Yeah."

"What's your address in St. Louis?"

After she provided the address and he plugged it into the app, a map of her old neighborhood was displayed. He set the phone camera to the opposite view and pointed it at his computer to show her the map.

"Do you remember how to get to the bank from your house?"

"Yes." She opened the map application on her own computer, duplicating the image shown on Griffin's. She scrolled through the map to the shopping center where the bank was located. Then she enlarged the map until individual business names began showing up on the map. The bank's name popped up. She pointed her phone's camera to her computer so Griffin could see. Then she clicked the bank icon to make it show street-view photos of the shopping center. She confirmed from the photos that the bank on the map was the bank she had remembered her parents using. It had branches all over the country, including in Cypress, Texas.

"Go get your money," Griffin said. "If I was there, I'd take you."

The next day, Sophie again took Alia to school, as she had the first two weeks of school and the day before. Afterward, Alia got demon driver Dina to drive her home, with a stop at the bank on the way. Alia stared at her phone the whole way, to avoid seeing the dangerous situations Dina had narrowly missed.

Since she didn't have a bank card, she had to go inside to a teller and show her driver's license. She withdrew the entire $613.47 that had been in her old savings account. Combined with the money she had earned from lawnmowing and working at Bullseye, she had enough for repairs with a couple hundred left over.

* * *

Ahmed Khalifi logged into his bank account as he did periodically, to make sure there were no unexpected transactions. The online banking app listed all his accounts and a credit card. A checking account; a savings account; a savings account for his older daughter, which had a small balance but which she had not used in years since getting married; and a savings account for his younger daughter, who had disappeared over a year ago.

For a while, he had friends stake out the house of her boyfriend to see if she was hiding out with him, but his friends reported no sign of her. Perhaps their earlier visit to the boyfriend before Alia disappeared had truly helped the boy understand that the cultural and religious differences between him and Alia were too great for the relationship to succeed.

At the banking app page that listed all the accounts, something caught Ahmed's attention. Alia's account showed a zero balance. He could have sworn it had six hundred dollars in it a few days ago. He clicked the link to open the account. The balance had been withdrawn the previous Monday. A quick discussion with his wife confirmed that she had been unaware of the missing money.

The next day, Ahmed visited the local branch of his bank to find out what happened to the money. With a few clicks of a mouse, the customer service representative determined that the entirety of the account, $613.47, was withdrawn at a branch in the small town of Cypress, Texas. Ahmed checked Google Maps to find that it was a suburb of Houston.

After exiting the bank, Ahmed called the police detective who had been investigating Alia's disappearance. "Detective Billings, this is Ahmed Khalifi. I think my daughter is in Texas. Last week she took out all the money from her savings account."

He proceeded to tell the detective of the connection to a suburb of Houston, Texas. He could hear the detective tapping on a computer keyboard.

"I'm checking our database for anything new," he explained. After what seemed like ages, he heard the detective suck in his breath.

"She – or someone – applied for a replacement driver's license with an address in Joplin. The license record had a note that she was a missing person, and whoever processed that license was supposed to contact us about it. Apparently, they didn't follow protocol. Mr. Khalifi, this could be nothing more than identity thieves exploiting a tragedy. I'll make some inquiries in Texas and let you know what I find."

* * *

Detective Billings called Mr. Khalifi the next afternoon.

"Mr. Khalifi, a few weeks after the new driver's license was issued, she also applied for a license in Texas. I checked the Texas police records and didn't find anything listed for her name. At least not at the state level.

"So I called someone in Houston who has access to Harris County records. Still nothing under your daughter's name, but then…ah… they offered to do a facial recognition check using her driver's license photo against the arrest photos in their system. If she used a different name, something might pop up."

"And did something pop up?"

"Yes. It's not comfortable to tell you, but… ah… there is an arrest record back in July for someone who looks very much like Alia. The date of birth she gave was the same, but with an earlier year, to make her seem older. The name in the report is 'Alicia Kelly'. It sounds sort of like Alia Khalifi, don't you think?"

"What was she arrested for?"

"This is the uncomfortable part. She was arrested for prostitution."

Detective Billings could hear moaning coming through the phone. "Mr. Khalifi? Are you alright?"

"No. My daughter is a prostitute."

"The charges were dropped. That's probably why they didn't pursue an identity check on the alias."

"So, she's not a prostitute?"

"I talked with the arresting officer. We're talking roughly ten months ago, but he remembered some details about the case. He said they raided a motel and picked up several girls and a few johns – men who were paying for sex. She was one of the girls."

"But the charges were dropped."

"The prosecutor wanted to concentrate on the men rather than the girls. One reason was a staff shortage among the police, another is the general belief in their department that the girls are victims and it's the johns who are the criminals."

"But it's possible Alia is not a prostitute," Ahmed hoped.

"Mr. Khalifi, I don't want to take away your optimism, but you have to be realistic. She was picked up at a motel with a group of prostitutes." Mr. Khalifi resumed moaning, then suddenly let loose a string of angrily spoken words in a language unfamiliar to Detective Billings. At least, the words sounded angry to the detective.

"Look at the positive aspect, Mr. Khalifi. Your daughter's alive and well enough to pass a driving test. You could still get a happy ending."

"What is her address?"

Chapter 23
He's here

Ahmed had been driving all day. He couldn't bring himself to tell his wife that their youngest daughter ran away to become a prostitute. He told her he was called away on a business trip. Only his closest friends knew what he had found out; the friends who held to the true tenets of their faith and whom Ahmed trusted not to tell others. They understood his shame and sympathized with his request for discretion. He left Sunday for his Monday "business meeting."

Ahmed arrived in Cypress after dark and drove by the address listed on Alia's driver's license. It looked like a middle-class suburban neighborhood, nicer than his own. Large houses, neatly trimmed lawns, most cars parked in driveways rather than on the street. The exception was a car parked in front of the target house. *Is this a brothel? Do the neighbors know?* he wondered. *They probably know and don't care. She had been arrested at a motel, so perhaps this is only a place to live, not to conduct her illicit business.*

He saw lights on in the house and occasional shadows move across a window. He almost dozed off when he heard voices. He saw a young man and woman leave the house. The woman was not Alia. The couple walked to the car parked on the street. After a brief hug, the woman got into the car and drove away as the man waved. The woman didn't appear to have been in any distress, so she was obviously there of her own will. *Is the man her pimp?* Ahmed didn't understand this sex business.

Soon a pink pickup with dark swirl designs pulled up in the driveway next to a dark-colored truck. He couldn't see who exited the vehicle, as the driver entered the house through the back door, remaining in shadows the entire time. He'd heard of pimps driving flashy cars. This pink truck with unusual custom designs seemed to fit the stereotype. He decided to leave before the earlier woman returned and noticed his car loitering on the street. He would return tomorrow to stake out the area.

* * *

Ahmed returned too late in the morning to see the residents. He assumed that prostitutes and their enablers were night people and would be sleeping late. He wanted to get there for his surveillance mission after the school buses had made their rounds and business people had left for work so as not to attract attention to himself. When he arrived back at the house, the vehicles were no longer in the driveway.

He pulled up next to the curb and looked around at the deserted street. He reached down to the mess on the floor in front of the passenger seat and grabbed a roll of duct tape. He peeled back the end slightly and placed the roll on the seat for easy access later. Then he opened the glove compartment and pulled out the handgun he had purchased years ago for protection. It was usually located in the nightstand beside his bed at home but might be necessary for this trip. He hoped the mere presence of it would be enough to instill cooperation in any who might see it, but he was prepared to demonstrate the severity of the situation, if necessary.

He walked up to the house and peered through the window by the door. He didn't see any movement inside. He rang the bell. Still no sign of activity. He walked back to the garage and tried the pedestrian door of the garage. It was unlocked. *So foolish.* He opened the door and saw a vast space big enough for two cars. Not filled with junk like so many garages. *That means there had been cars here, but they were now gone.* He had missed his opportunity to get his daughter. He would have to stake out the house for their eventual return.

In mid-afternoon, Ahmed watched a lawn crew mowing a lawn down the street. Their beat-up truck and dark complexions didn't give him nearly the concern that the appearance of a homeowner would. They were background noise.

Eventually, he saw a teenaged Black girl get off of a school bus and walk to the house. *She looks so normal. They are recruiting schoolgirls. But that is what Alia is. Or was. It is sad.* A half-hour later, the pink truck returned. It pulled up into the driveway and this time, Ahmed could see the driver. It was Alia; dressed in clothing that showed her bare arms and legs. His anger rose at the sight. She had left behind the customs of her faith and culture. Ahmed had expected that, but it still made him angry. Did she return from conducting her business elsewhere in broad daylight? Perhaps at the motel Detective Billings had mentioned? Or did she come back to prepare for her customers here in this house?

Ahmed drove closer and pulled up again to the curb in front of the house and repeated the steps he had taken in the morning. The duct tape lay on the front passenger seat. The doors were left unlocked for easy access. The gun tucked into his waistband, covered by his shirt. He glanced down at the machete on the floor. He would not need that yet.

Emi and Alia both heard the pounding on the door, but Emi was closest. She saw a frowning man with pinched eyebrows standing at the door. He saw her too. He tried to open the locked door but could only rattle it.

"I'm here for Alia," he snarled. "Open this door!"

Alia peered down from her perch at the top of the stairs and gasped at the sight. "It's my father! Don't let him in!"

Emi looked back at Mr. Khalifi and shouted back, "No! Alia doesn't want to see you. Go away!"

"Unlock this door!"

"No!"

Ahmed took out his gun, held it by the barrel, and used it as a hammer to break the window to the right of the door. He

249

switched his gun to the left hand and reached through the window with his right to unlock the door. With the gun hand, he pressed the latch and pushed the door open, then switched the gun back to his right hand.

Emi backed away while Alia seemed to be frozen at the top of the stairs.

Ahmed waved the gun from Emi to Alia and back to Emi. "Alia! Come down now! You're coming with me!

Alia retreated to the bedroom and slammed the door. She dialed 9-1-1.

"Alia! Come down now! I have no problem shooting your little prostitute friend here, but I won't have to do that if you come with me."

When Ahmed's attention had turned to his daughter, Emi escaped through the kitchen and crouched below the bar separating the kitchen and informal dining room. She dialed 9-1-1. At the sound of the emergency operator, Emi whispered, "A man with a gun is trying to kidnap Alia. He said he would shoot me if she doesn't go with him." She provided the house address.

Alia emerged from her bedroom with tears streaming down her face. "Don't hurt Emi." She began walking down the stairs. "I don't want to go with you," she cried hoarsely. "This is my home now."

Emi ran out the back door to the garage while Ahmed grabbed ahold of his daughter with his free hand and dragged her to his car. He looked down the street to the lawn crew. One member was finishing up with a noisy leaf blower while another had just finished stowing away their other equipment in the trailer behind their aging truck. They were oblivious to the activity at the Jensen house. He shoved Alia to the ground and planted his knee on her back to keep her from escaping. He put his gun back into his waistband before binding Alia's wrists together behind her back with the duct tape. Once bound, he opened the back door of the car, lifted her off the ground by her armpits, shoved her in, and closed the door.

Alia's crying took on more definition. Between sobs she spoke, "God help me." After a gulp of air, she added, "This is my S-O-S."

"You have dishonored our family. How can you expect Allah to help you now?"

Louder, she cried out, "Jesus, I need you now. Help me!"

As Ahmed put the car into gear, the lawn truck slowly passed by, presumably off to its next job. The gate of the trailer fell open and made a loud scraping, screeching noise as it dragged on the concrete street. One of the mowers rolled out onto the street and the driver pulled the truck over slightly to the right in front of Ahmed to park. Both lawn men got out to attend to the errant trailer. Ahmed was blocked in.

Emi came barreling around the corner of the house holding a spray can in her right hand. Upon reaching the car, she held out the can and sprayed black paint over the windshield, blocking the driver's view.

Ahmed got out, enraged. First the lawn truck, now the paint. As he raised the gun to a menacing position, Emi sprayed him in the face. He screamed in pain as he was temporarily blinded by the paint.

John pulled up and parked in front of the neighbor's house, wondering at the strange sight of a lawn truck blocking access to his own house and a car with a black smear on the windshield parked in front. Emi was still holding the spray can.

"What's going on?" he called out as he got out of his vehicle. Only when walked closer did he see the man holding a gun. The man also had a black stripe across his eyes like a raccoon.

"He's trying to kidnap Alia!" Emi screamed.

John picked up speed and ran straight to the raccoon-faced man. He raised his arm and balled up his fist. At the right moment, he landed a punch on Ahmed's jaw while running at full speed. Ahmed dropped his gun and was knocked to the ground a few feet from where he had been standing. John nearly stumbled as his momentum carried him over the raccoon man's body. Emi kicked the gun under the car.

The first sheriff's deputy arrived in time to see Ahmed hit the ground. Another deputy pulled up moments later with a constable following right behind.

John ran around to the passenger side of the car to get Alia out of the back seat. The door wouldn't open.

"Emi, hit the unlock button!"

Emi stepped around Alia's father and pressed the button to unlock all the doors. John helped Alia out of the car. She ran to the house and crouched in the flower bed behind a row of bushes. John followed her to remove the duct tape from her hands.

Deputy Mike Guerrero approached Ahmed's car with his gun drawn and yelled "Hands up!" The lawn men raised their hands above their heads.

Emi pointed at Ahmed, laying on the ground, and shouted, "He tried to kidnap Alia."

Deputy Guerrero again shouted, "Hands up!"

From his position by the house, John raised his hands and shouted, "Emi! Put your hands up!"

Emi raised her hands and said more calmly, "He tried to kidnap Alia." She pointed with her chin to Ahmed, who was beginning to sit up.

Deputy Jessica Bell ran toward the group with her gun drawn. When she reached Deputy Guerrero, he holstered his gun and got out his handcuffs. Within a few seconds, he had Ahmed lying face down on the street with his hands cuffed behind his back.

Ahmed moaned that his eyes were burning.

As Deputy Bell holstered her sidearm, Emi, John and the lawn men lowered their hands. "Who's Alia?" Deputy Bell asked.

Emi pointed to the girl hiding behind a bush.

Constable Jimmy O'Neill began taking statements from the lawn men. Upon asking their names, one of the men pointed to the sign on the door of the truck. The sign said, "Ruiz Brothers Lawn Care." Below that were two first names, side by side, each with a phone number under it.

"You two are the Ruiz brothers?"

"Yes."

Constable O'Neill pointed to the names under the title. "Which one are you?"

* * *

By the time Ty and Sophie each made it home after John's calls, an ambulance had already taken Ahmed to the hospital for a possible broken jaw and eye injury and the law officers had already gotten the statements of everyone present.

A gloved inspector from the Harris County Sheriff's Department went through evidence in Ahmed's car while a tow truck waited to take it away. Ty noticed a handgun and a roll of duct tape each inside a clear plastic evidence bag laying on the hood of the car. Emi's spray paint was in another bag. The inspector was looking for a larger bag for a machete. The hairs on the back of Ty's neck stood up and he turned to Sophie. She responded by leaning closer to Ty and he put his arm around her.

"What's that big knife for?" Sophie asked quietly.

She didn't expect an answer, but the inspector had heard her question. "It looks like he bought it recently," the inspector stated. "The price tag's still attached. I doubt he was planning to cut brush with it."

Sophie took a deep breath and let it out slowly. "Let's go see Alia." They headed into the house.

Chapter 24
Everyone knows

"Earlier today, eighteen-year-old Alia Khalifi had just arrived home from school when her estranged father tried to kidnap her at this house in Cypress." The news reporter indicated the house behind her. "Alia had become a victim of sex trafficking after running away from home a year and a half ago. She has been living with a family in Cypress for the past several months while trying to reestablish her life.

"The father she had run away from had driven from St. Louis with questionable motives. He tried to kidnap Alia at gunpoint, but the quick-thinking actions of her fourteen-year-old host sister thwarted his efforts. Little Emily Jensen sprayed black paint on the windshield of his car blocking his view and then she sprayed his face when he got out of the car. Her heroic action stalled Mr. Khalifi's escape long enough for law enforcement to arrive and place him under arrest.

"Ahmed Khalifi is being held on federal kidnapping charges. Our sources within the FBI say attempted murder could be added as they found a newly purchased machete in his vehicle. The case is still under investigation.

"This is Dominique Evans, reporting live from Cypress."

* * *

"She called me 'little'. I'm fourteen, not seven," Emi complained, upon watching the replay of the newscast on TV.

"At least you got a mention. She didn't say anything about me knocking Mr. Khalifi down," John added.

"I need to buy another Rescue Hero shirt for Emi," Alia said, trying to lend some humor to the situation. Her voice still wavered from the emotion of the afternoon, and she continued holding a teddy bear she had taken from the collection on the fireplace mantle. News of the machete had been another shock.

Emi went to the fireplace, picked up another teddy bear, walked back to Alia, and sat next to her on the sofa. "Let's swap the bears," Emi said, gently tugging on the one Alia held and offering up the other.

"Why?"

"Because the one you're holding is you, so it's like you're hugging yourself. This one is me."

"I don't understand."

"You mean no one told you about the bears?"

"I thought they were just cute decorations and maybe one of you was a collector or something."

"We started the collection after our parents died. Lots of people brought us teddy bears along with flowers and cards for the funeral." Emi stood up and pointed. "Those two up on that high shelf by the fireplace represent Mom and Dad. Those on the mantle represent our family, including you. Except now you're holding my bear and I'm holding yours." She walked back to the fireplace and set the Alia bear on the mantle with the other family bears.

Alia followed Emi to the mantle. She gathered up the bear family and squeezed them together in a tight hug. Then she placed them all back on the mantle.

"Lizzie's here," Sophie called out. "It looks like she brought food." Lizzie carried a jug of lemonade and a bag of food from a local chicken restaurant.

"Good. It was my turn to cook," Ty stated, "and I don't feel much like cooking."

"You didn't need to anyway. Mrs. Burr called to say she would bring over a casserole," Sophie added.

John and Emi had already rehashed their stories to several neighbors over the last couple of hours. The kids on the block came over while the deputies were still investigating. And after the kids' parents arrived home, a new wave of neighbors came by.

* * *

Alia:
School seemed surreal
today.

When school started, most of
the kids didn't know anything
about what happened
yesterday. But when
teachers said they would
give me extra time to turn in
my homework, the news
spread.

I saw some kids looking at
their phones and then
looking at me. I don't want to
be a celebrity. Not for that.

And the worst part is now
everyone knows I was a
prostitute.

> Andy:
> The news report said 'sex
> trafficking victim'.

What difference does it
make? Everyone knows
what I did.

I don't even know how the
news people figured out I'm
a 'sex trafficking victim'. I
mean, the only time I ever
dealt with the police, I gave
them a fake name and they
eventually let me go.

Are you going to hide out?

No point now. I've already
been to school.

And I don't want to miss
classes. It would be too hard
to make up the work.

I wish I could be there with
you right now. Maybe this
weekend?

I don't know. I promised to
mow some of John's lawns
on Saturday so he can do a
service project with Ty.

And then I have a shift at
Bullseye in the evening.

So, you were almost
kidnapped, but it's life as
usual? You're stronger than
me.

But quieter and not as funny.

Well, that was funny.

* * *

Cathy Rutherford:

I just want you to know we're
praying for you.

Alia:
Thx. I don't know if Mrs.
Cortez will let me help with
the toddlers anymore after
this.

You know my story and they
let me teach kindergarten.

Let me know if there's
anything specific I can help
you with.

Okay. Thx.

* * *

Caleb:
Mom told me what
happened. I just want you to
know if you need anything,
I'll be there for you.

*You weren't there when I needed you a few months ago. Why should
I believe you now?*

Alia:
Thx

* * *

Griffin:
Hi Alia.
When you told us things
were bad with your dad, I
had no idea how bad.

I'm so sorry you went
through that. I want to help.
What can I do?

Alia:
I can't think of anything. I just
appreciate that you thought
about me. And didn't cut me
off.

That's crazy. Who would do
something like that?

* * *

News outlets in St. Louis picked up the story out of Houston
and added their local spin, with a mention of Alia's former high
school. Alia's old friends and classmates had always wondered
what had happened to her. Some thought her parents had sent
her off to the Muslim equivalent of a convent.

"If her father was pissed at her dating a non-Muslim, he
must have been super pissed at this," former classmate Elena
stated. "Are you sure you didn't know anything about it,
Conner? After all, you guys were dating."

"I thought they might've sent her to an all-girls boarding school, but I'd hoped she somehow got out on her own. I just didn't expect sex trafficking."

"Yeah, instead of banging one guy, she must've been banging hundreds."

"Shut up, Cameron," Elena said.

"Yeah, shut up," Conner echoed. "You don't know the whole story."

"And what is the story?"

"One day, when I just got home from school, these two dudes showed up. They told me if I cared for Alia, I wouldn't go out with her or talk to her again. If I kept on seeing her, it could put her life in danger. Not *my* life in danger, but *her* life."

"What'd they look like? Like mafia hitmen?" Cameron asked.

"I don't know what a mafia hitman would look like. These guys had beards and talked with a middle east accent. I didn't know if they were bluffing or not, so I broke up with her."

"You need to tell that to the FBI," Elena said. "Like, seriously."

* * *

The teddy bears that Alia had been holding after the kidnapping made their way back to the mantle, but the one that Emi had placed in her bed on her first night found its way back into her bed after sitting on the dresser for several months. *I'm eighteen years old and I'm sleeping with a teddy bear. Is that okay?*

* * *

On Saturday afternoon, upon returning from mowing lawns, Alia found that she had visitors. They had been sitting on the sofa chatting with Sophie and Emi but stood up when Alia walked in the door.

"Alia," the older woman simply said.

Alia froze while an emotional surge built up within her.

"Mama, what are you doing here?"

"I wanted to see you. To see that you are alive; not lost. I cried for weeks when you left." She stepped forward to hug Alia.

"Mama, I'm sweaty."

"I don't care. I missed you so much." She put her arms around Alia.

After an awkward moment with her arms by her side, Alia finally wrapped her arms around her mother. Then the flood of tears began. Alia's sister Alma joined in a group hug. Sophie and Emi retreated to their bedrooms.

"We were all so worried about you," Alma said.

"I'm sorry I made everyone worried. I'm sorry I ran away." After another minute of the tearful hug, Alia stated, "But I'm not sorry that Baba's in jail."

"They added attempted murder to his charges. They said he planned to kill you," her mother said. "I could not believe it. I came to see you but I also wanted to hear from your father's own mouth what he intended. I saw him this morning."

"And?"

"He denies that he wanted to kill you. He said he just wanted to bring you home."

"He pointed a gun at a fourteen-year-old girl and said he would shoot her if I didn't go with him. Then he tied me up. That's not what a father does. A father loves his children and celebrates if he finds one that had been lost. I have no love for him. Not back in St. Louis and certainly not now."

"He does love you. He just doesn't show it well."

"He was terrible to us. You, Alma, me. He was abusive; treated you like you were stupid. I think you have Stockholm syndrome."

"What is that?"

Alma explained, "Mama, it's when hostages eventually sympathize with their captors. It's a coping mechanism."

"You should have left him a long time ago and taken us with you," Alia stated.

"But he is your father."

"Not anymore. I have to get ready for work."

"I thought you just came from working."

"I mow lawns in the morning and this evening I'm working at a department store."

"They make you work so much."

"This family doesn't make me work. They pay for everything I need. I work for myself."

"I hope you will come back home with us."

"This is my home. With this family."

"Alia…."

"You should divorce Baba and go live with Alma."

Just then John and Ty came in from their service project of helping elderly church members.

"Hi," John said in greeting the two guests wearing hijabs.

"John, Ty, meet my mother and sister. Mrs. Leila Khalifi and Alma."

"Hey," John said in greeting.

"It's nice to meet you," Ty said. "I'd shake hands, but I'm still a bit dirty."

"They're just leaving. I have to shower and get ready for my shift at the store."

Upon hearing the front door close, Sophie emerged from her room to see Alia going upstairs and her mother and sister standing outside on the front walkway. She had heard the whole conversation from her bedroom. She passed Ty on his way to the bedroom as she went to the front door and stepped outside.

"Mrs. Khalifi, I'm sorry the visit didn't go as well as you expected."

"I didn't know what to expect."

"I want you to know she is doing well here. She has friends. She's going to school, she's working at a department store, and she's mowing lawns. That's her truck." Sophie pointed at the truck backed into the driveway. "She bought it with the money she earned from mowing lawns and working at the store. She even painted it herself. This may not be the lifestyle you wanted for her, but she's safe and cared for."

"Thank you."

"Give her time. This has been a traumatic event for her, for all of us. I'm sure she'll eventually want to see you."

"I don't agree with what she did – running away – but I understand why," Alma said. Her mother looked at her in surprise.

"Alma!"

"I agree with Alia that you should've divorced Baba a long time ago. Someone should have stood up to him. I was just too cowardly to do it. I want you to come live with us and help with the baby. I don't think Baba's coming back for a long time."

A car pulled up to the curb.

"Mrs. Khalifi, it looks like your ride is here. It was nice meeting you both. And give Alia more time."

Chapter 25
The names

Upon arrival at church, someone stepped in front of her path as Alia was about to enter the doorway.

"Sorry," she said as she almost bumped into him.

"Can I have your autograph?" the guy said.

Alia hadn't paid attention to the guy's face before he spoke.

"Andy? What are you doing here?"

"And Shelby," Andy said, pointing to his cousin standing next to him.

"And he's still socially awkward," Shelby commented. "Autograph? Are you serious?" She swatted him on the arm.

"You kind of dismissed me from seeing you yesterday, so I had to come here today," Andy explained. "This has been a big week for you and I'm sorry I couldn't be here for you."

"Thank you. I didn't know you were a church person."

"I go sometimes."

"Yeah, when you know some pretty girl will be there," Shelby stated.

"Like now?" he replied, looking at Alia. "Maybe we should add 'courageous and capable girl' to that description."

"Come on," Ty urged. "If we want to sit together, we need to get seats before they're all taken."

Alia sat between Andy and Shelby when the music began, prompting them to stand. Another person joined their row, standing next to Shelby. He leaned over and said, "Hi Alia," in a whisper loud enough to be heard over the music.

"Griffin! I didn't know you came here on Sunday mornings."

"I usually don't, but I heard a local celebrity would be here."

"Who?"

"You."

"See," Andy said, also in a loud whisper. "I tried to get her autograph and she refused." Andy held his fist out towards Griffin in expectation of a fist bump. "I'm Andy." Griffin returned with a fist bump."

"Griffin goes to my pizza group on Sunday nights," Alia explained.

"Hey," Griffin said in greeting.

"Andy and Shelby don't usually go here either. They're freshmen at A&M and are back for the weekend."

"I'm a freshman at Blinn," Griffin told Shelby.

Shelby put her arm behind Griffin's back and pulled him over to switch places with her so he could sit next to the celebrity and not have to talk/whisper across her.

"Oh, sorry," Griffin said.

"Don't worry about it," Shelby replied, patting his arm.

A woman on the row behind them leaned forward and said, "shh."

After the service, Alia explained to Andy, Shelby, and Griffin that she couldn't stay with them as she would be helping with the toddler class. *That is, if they let me,* she thought to herself.

"That's okay," Andy said. "Ty and Sophie invited us for lunch, so we'll see you at your house later."

Alia shrugged apologetically to Griffin. She considered inviting Griffin for lunch but knew Andy liked her and she wasn't sure if she should squelch that affection; wasn't even sure she wanted to squelch it. Andy was sometimes annoying, but he was growing on her.

As they were about to part ways, Griffin leaned in and whispered in Alia's ear. She smiled and nodded in reply.

On the way from the worship service to the preschool hallway of the church, Alia passed the room designated as the 'counseling center'. At the end of every worship service, the pastor invited anyone who wanted to join the church or make a decision about Christ to go to the counseling center, a large room with several clusters of tables and chairs. This time she paused to look in and saw a young couple with a small child at one table with a church volunteer and a single woman talking with a volunteer at another table. A man in the room with a name tag noticed her and began walking toward her. She quickly turned away and headed to the toddler room.

Mrs. Cortez let Alia help with the toddlers as usual. If she'd heard about Alia's story, she made no mention of it.

* * *

"What did that guy whisper to you after the service?" Emi asked on the ride home.

"I'm not sure. He either invited me to get frozen yogurt after tonight's Bible study or asked for Shelby's phone number."

"Yeah, right. I saw you nodding. Are you going?"

"Yes."

* * *

Andy and Shelby returned to A&M in the late afternoon. Alia made a conscious effort to maintain her normal routine as she had been all week. However, at Paolo's Pizza that evening, she was more subdued than usual upon greeting the group. The meeting started with an unusual statement from Shakir.

"Alia, I've been praying for you."

"Thank you. Are you a Christian now?"

"I don't know. I've been thinking about it a lot, but, as I said before, it's hard to leave behind my culture."

"Well, it's not hard for me," Alia said. "I think I'm a Christian now. I'm not sure what I'm supposed to do about it."

"Alia, that's great!" Cathy said. "Have you told anyone?"

"You guys are the first."

"Later I can tell you how to make it official with the church," Cathy stated.

"I can see how you'd be able to dump the stuff that's holding me back," Shakir said.

"Can you tell us what happened?" Shell asked.

"I mean, we saw the news clip, but it didn't go into details," Griffin added.

She recounted the details of her father's visit, his threat against Emi, and his duct taping her wrists behind her back.

"I was scared for Emi, and scared for myself. When I was sitting in the car, I just started praying. I prayed to Allah, then I switched and prayed in Jesus' name. I just knew if my father drove away, no one would see me again. But then I heard this screeching sound and looked up and a lawn truck stopped next to us and blocked us in. I remember seeing the sign on the side of the truck: 'Ruiz Brothers Lawn Care'.

"And when I saw the brothers' names under that, I knew God had answered my prayer. I know Emi and John did some things to help the police arrest my father, but I wasn't paying attention to that. They had to tell me later."

"Why would the lawn men's names have such an impact on you?" Shakir asked.

"Their names were Jesus and Angel."

"It's probably pronounced 'Heh-soos'," Bobby corrected.

* * *

As the participants of the pizza Bible study dispersed to their various vehicles for the evening, Griffin looked at Alia. "Are you still up for frozen yogurt?"

Alia nodded, "Sure."

"I have a question about Monday."

"What?"

"Did you get Jesus' phone number? 'Cause I have a lot of questions for him."

Alia laughed. "If I had his number, I don't think I'd need these meetings anymore." Then she added, "But if you just need someone to mow your lawn, I could help with that."

Chapter 26
Mother's Day

Friday afternoon, Alia made a stop on her way home from school. Mother's Day was on Sunday and a grocery store on the way had a tent in the parking lot from which it sold flowers and cards. She purchased a bouquet of colorful flowers and a card.

When Sophie came in from college later, she immediately noticed the vase of flowers sitting in the middle of the kitchen table. A card in a lavender envelope with her name on it leaned against the vase. Sophie smiled at the sight but was still puzzled as to the occasion. Ty hadn't arrived home yet and, besides, the handwriting on the envelope looked feminine.

She called out to the household. "Who's home?"

"We're all home, doing homework," John responded.

"What are the flowers for?"

"What flowers?" John responded again.

"The ones on the table."

Ty pulled up as she was about to ask about the flowers again. As Ty entered the house, Alia came out of her room and said, "The flowers are from me."

Alia made her way downstairs as Ty asked, "What's the occasion?"

Alia picked up the card and handed it to Sophie. "Open it."

Dear Sophie,

Happy Mother's Day

You may not be my mother, more like a sister, but you're the mother of this house. You welcomed me and you made me feel loved. Thank you for letting me in.

I love you,

Alia

"Oh, Alia. This is beautiful. Thank you. I love you, too."

By this time Emi and John made their way down to see the flowers. Sophie passed around the card.

"Can we have a family game night tonight?" Alia asked.

"I'm open to that," Ty stated.

"I planned to hang out with Lizzie, but I'm sure she'd like to do a game night," John added.

"Can I pick the game?" Emi asked.

* * *

"Ty said you adopted him before you got married," Alia said at dinner Monday night. "Can you really adopt a grown-up?"

"It wasn't a legal adoption, but we just wanted him to know that he was part of our family," Sophie explained.

"Can I be part of your family?"

"Yes," Ty said almost before Alia had completed her sentence. The others smiled at his quick response and nodded.

Sophie reached for Alia's hand. "You're already part of the family, and I think we all just agreed to adopt you."

"Does she get a poster, too?" Ty directed at Emi.

"Oh yeah! I'll make it tonight."

John cleared his throat. "You know," he began. "There is such a thing as adult adoption. We could make it legal."

"What do you mean? I'm already grown up," Alia pointed out.

"When I was researching about having Ty be another legal guardian for me and Emi, I found something about adult adoption. At first, I thought it was just symbolic, but I found out it means you would legally become Ty's and Sophie's dependent, like for tax deductions and insurance."

"John, download the documents and find out what we need to do," Ty directed.

Epilogue

Early July

"Alia, you got a letter. It looks official," Emi called out.

"Is it from school?" Alia asked as she came downstairs.

"No. I think it's your new driver's license."

Alia took the letter and poked her finger under the edge of the flap to tear it open.

"Look," she said, holding out her license for Emi to see. "I'm official."

"You've been official for weeks."

"Well, this makes it double official."

She stared at the name on the license and smiled.

Alia Rahab Jentler.

The End

Acknowledgments

I want to thank my wife Wendy for her feedback with the story and encouragement to complete this project and my daughter Katie who was my first reviewer and provided the earliest advice.

For those reviewers outside of my family, my thanks go once again to my neighbor Cassie C. for reviewing an early draft and recommending improvements.

I also want to acknowledge a YouTube video about an incoherent young woman who tried to get into a stranger's car at a gas station in Albuquerque, New Mexico in October 2016. After seeing the video, I wondered who she was and what happened to her. My story is entirely fictional and in no way represents the real people in the video, but I acknowledge that the video sparked the creative juices that culminated in this story of Alia.

The YouTube video can be viewed at the following URL: https://www.youtube.com/watch?v=P_qXE_fXquY&t=75s Note that the video includes rough language.

About the Author

Todd H. Davis is the father of three kids (two girls and a boy) who were older teenagers at the time of writing *The Trailer Behind the Garage* and its sequel, *The Gas Station Girl*. He lives with his "smarter-than-me" wife in the Houston, Texas, suburb of Cypress, which is the setting for his novels.

Todd spent most of his life in the Houston area, except for the two years in Japan as a young man, teaching English in churches in the Nagasaki area. While he was getting used to Asian culture, his wife, who had recently arrived in the US from China for studies, was getting used to American culture. They have spent the time since then getting used to each other.

You can contact him through his website:

www.toddhdavis.com

Books by Todd H. Davis

The Trailer Behind the Garage

The Gas Station Girl

The Lingering Scent of Wrong Assumptions

The DollarFly Girls
a prequel to The Gas Station Girl

Coming soon:
The Kennedi Identity

www.ingramcontent.com/pod-product-compliance
Lightning Source LLC
Chambersburg PA
CBHW020244180626
46810CB00006B/2360